SH

F. ORLD WAR

Edited by George Bruce

SIDGWICK AND JACKSON
LONDON

First published in U.K. by
Sidgwick and Jackson Limited, 1971

ISBN 0 283 48460 8

Printed in Great Britain by
The Anchor Press Ltd., Tiptree, Essex
for
Sidgwick and Jackson Limited
1 Tavistock Chambers, Bloomsbury Way
London, WC1

CONTENTS

ACKNOWLEDGMENTS

RICHARD ALDINGTON, 'At all Costs'. Reprinted by kind permission of Madame Catherine Guillanne, from *Roads to Glory*.

JOHN BUCHAN, 'The King of Ypres'. Reprinted by kind permission of The Tweedsmuir Trustees.

H. M. TOMLINSON, 'All our Yesterdays'. Reprinted by kind permission of The Society of Authors as the literary representative of the Estate of H. M. Tomlinson.

'BARTIMEUS' (Lewis Anselm da Costa Ricci), 'Battle of the Mist'. Reprinted by kind permission of Dr. Ritchie and Messrs. Cassell, from *The Long Trick*.

'SAPPER' (Lieutenant-Colonel H. C. McNeile), 'The Mine'. Reprinted by kind permission of the trustees of the late Colonel H. C. McNeile (Sapper) and Hodder and Stoughton, from *Sapper's War Stories*.

C. E. MONTAGUE, 'A Trade Report Only'. Reprinted by kind permission of Mrs. Rose Elton and Chatto and Windus, from *Fiery Particles*.

ERNEST RAYMOND, 'The Debris'. Reprinted by kind permission of the author, from *The Jesting Army*.

LORD DUNSANY (Edward John Moreton Drax Plunkett, 18th Baron), 'The Prayer of the Men of Daleswood'. Reprinted by kind permission of Ernest Benn Limited, from *Tales of War*.

'TAFFRAIL' (Captain H. T. Dorling, R.N.), 'The Night Patrol'. Reprinted by kind permission of Mr. J. J. Dorling and Messrs. Chambers, from *A Little Ship*.

FRANCIS BRETT YOUNG, 'Marching on Tanga'. Reprinted by kind permission of Collins Publishers.

IAN HAY (Sir John Hay Beith), 'The Last Solo'. Reprinted by kind permission of The Owners of the Copyright and William Blackwood Limited, from *Carrying On After The First 100,000*.

SIR HERBERT READ, 'Killed in Action'. Reprinted by kind permission of the Author and Hogarth Press, from *Ambush: Criterion Miscellany, No. 16*.

SHORT STORIES OF THE FIRST WORLD WAR

FOREWORD

This anthology is composed of either fiction or reportage – and here the dividing line between the two is narrow – about the First World War, August 1914 to November 1918, by British writers who took part in it on land or at sea. All of them survived the war, though none were armchair writers remote from the fighting. The omission of a number of writers will indicate that it is a representative rather than a comprehensive anthology: representative in that it reflects the kind of work war writers were producing at that time, as well as the national values and attitudes that gave rise to their writing.

The First World War created a watershed in British writing, the decisive event being the first Battle of the Somme, 1 July to 18 November 1916, when the British lost 420,000 men, the French 195,000, and the Germans 650,000. Before this battle, patriotic jingoism still cloaked the war in glory and heroism, of which the peak was either victory or *pro patria mori*.

But after the catastrophe of this battle, mass hypnotism, or romantic nationalism, or whatever, seems to have come to an abrupt end. Few of the fighting men appear to have gone on believing in the sanity of their leaders; appeals to patriotism and the Almighty fell upon ever more deaf ears; cynicism and a dogged, bitter determination to hold on under the iron pressure of military discipline became the norm. The best of the war writers reflected this changed mood, as they writhed beneath artillery barrages that exploded above them ceaselessly for three days or more; or stumbled with their battalions through the shambles of No Man's Land into the murderous machine-gun fire which protected the enemy positions.

A rigid censorship of letters from the front line and of war correspondents' reports suppressed all but meaningless clichés and the fog of official communiqués, and, we may remind ourselves, there were no television and news-reel cameras at hand to reveal the widespread horror. Writers, or at least some of them, felt compelled to tell the world what was really going on around them and what their innermost reactions to it were.

The writers fall roughly into two categories: those who accepted the war and its consequences without reserve because of blind patriotism; and those who became increasingly critical of how it was being fought, as well as its huge cost in human life and human values. This, then, was the watershed, the entry for the first time of naked realism based upon literary skill into our national battle literature; for, apart from a few volumes of memoirs from the Napoleonic Wars and from British India, in which adherence to brute fact outweighed literary skill, this quality was unknown there.

More important, this First World War literature opened doors to new values as well as new vistas of language, subject, and content, and this was not encouraged by the Establishment. The movement spread and has grown and developed ever since, though not perhaps with altogether desirable results. But the writers of the First World War had to force open the doors to prevent the horrors of twentieth-century war being glossed over and lost to humanity.

The writers included in this anthology are representative of both the 'patriotic' and the questioning, as well as some who fall into neither category. Ian Hay (Major Beith) reflected the glowing patriotism of 1914 to 1916, becoming, to judge from the numerous editions of his books, a wartime literary phenomenon. He wrote of a war fit for heroes, hardly ever moving far from this groove. Who but a strait-jacketed Establishment writer could possibly refer to the 'wine of success' in relation to the Somme? Yet his writing, always graphic and economical, is representative of the time.

Another who accepted the First World War situation without question was 'Sapper' (Major H. C. McNeile), who became famous for war stories based interestingly upon the belief that anyone beyond the pale of the British upper classes was a fool, a villain, or a joke; and *The Mine* is a fair example of this attitude. Sapper's stories, which exploited this idea again and again for a solid middle-class audience, also ran into numerous reprints, and no doubt inspired many young and some older officers with an uncritical belief in their own infallibility.

All too different was Richard Aldington, whose corrosive bitterness permeates *At All Costs*, a piece of writing of great impact describing what seems to have been an all too common situation then: a corps or divisional general in some comfortable château behind the lines issues an order to troops on the under-manned front to stand fast and die under the advancing enemy juggernaut. For its compression, its characterization, and its economy of method it is also outstanding.

Similar in its bitterness about war, but different in method is H. M. Tomlinson's *A Dream*. By a great effort of detachment, an intellectual feat, he depicts the war scene from the standpoint of a man totally ignorant of it who suddenly arrives where shell-bursts and violent death are commonplace. Nightmarish, surrealistic even, its lesson is that war is lunatic. Ernest Raymond's *The Debris*, and Herbert Read's *Killed In Action*, in different ways both depict the fate of men for whom, despite their dogged hold on themselves, war becomes overwhelming. By contrast, Francis Brett Young, in an account nearer to reportage than fiction, experiences spiritual exultation at the splendour of his surroundings when threatened by imminent death during a retreat in the East African bush. But he had not known the slow painful death of the spirit in months of trench warfare.

Neither of the two writers of war at sea, 'Taffrail' (Captain H. T. Dorling, R.N.) and 'Bartimeus' (L. A. da Costa Ricci), both of whom were famous in their day, were affected by the disillusionment with the war, probably because of professionalism, and the fact that naval experience was centuries old. Since the time of Queen Elizabeth I, British sailors had been keeping the sea lanes clear of the enemy, giving and receiving hurricanes of shot and shell the while. But both of these stories of the war at sea are distinguished by stark realism. *Battle of the Mist*, a semi-fictional account of the Battle of Jutland, and *Night Patrol*, which depicts the truth behind an official communiqué, are matter-of-fact, unvarnished stories of the incredible violence of sea warfare.

But, for the British and the Americans especially, war is not only and always grim and earnest; humour and laughter help to ease tensions, take the edge off trying situations, and help men at war to try to stay human. Sometimes, in proportion to the grimness of the situation, the laughter can be a little oriental. I recall a soldier in Malaya hitting a wasp nest with his hand when signalling down a helicopter. The wasps chased him round the jungle clearing and the entire party of troops collapsed with laughter. I have included two stories, one by John Buchan, the other by C. E. Montague, which in contrasting ways reflect this taste for extracting laughter out of a trying situation; and one by Lord Dunsany, half humour and half his own particular kind of sentiment.

GEORGE BRUCE

To All ranks of the British Forces in France

Three weeks ago today the Enemy began his terrific attacks against us on a 50 mile front. His objects are to separate us from the French, to take the Channel ports and destroy the British Army.

In spite of throwing already 106 Divisions into the battle and ~~suffering~~ enduring the most reckless sacrifice of human life, he has as yet made little progress towards his goals.

We owe this to the determined fighting & self sacrifice of our troops. Words fail me to express the admiration which I feel for the splendid resistance offered by all ranks of our army under the most trying circumstances.

Many amongst us now are ~~[illegible]~~ tired. To those I would say that Victory will belong to the side which holds out the longest. The French army is moving rapidly & in great force to our support - - - -

There is no other course open to us but to fight it out! Every position must be held to the last man: there must be no retirement. With our backs to the wall, and believing in the justice of our cause each one of us must fight on to the end. The safety of our Homes and the Freedom of mankind alike depend upon the conduct of each one of us at this critical moment. ~~But be of good cheer, the British Empire must win in the end.~~

D. Haig. F.M.

Thursday 11 April 1918

AT ALL COSTS

Richard Aldington

'Blast!'

Captain Hanley, commanding 'B' Company, stumbled over a broken duckboard and fell forward against the side of the trench. His tilted helmet shielded his face, but the trench wall felt oozy and soggy to his naked hand as he tried to steady himself.

'Mind that hole, Parker.'

'Very good, sir.'

He felt wet mud soaking through his breeches above the short gum boots, and his right sleeve was wet to the elbow. He fumbled in his gas bag, also wet with slimy mud, to see that the mask goggles were unbroken. O.K., but he swore again with a sort of exasperated groan over the crashing bruise on his right knee.

'Are you 'it, sir?'

'No, I only fell in that mucking hole again. I've told the ser'ant-

Field-Marshal Haig's orders for the day, dated Thursday 11 April 1918.

major umpteen times to get it mended. One of these days the brigadier'll fall into it and then there'll be hell to pay. Help me find my torch. I hope the bloody thing isn't broken.'

The two men groped in the darkness, fingering the slimy mud and tilted broken duckboards. Suddenly they crashed helmets.

'Sorry, sir.'

'All right, sorry.'

'Doesn't seem to be 'ere, sir.'

'Never mind, we'll look for it in the morning.'

They stumbled on cautiously. The trench was very deep (old German communication), very dark, very shell-smashed, very muddy. A black, heavy-clouded night, about an hour before dawn. Occasionally a strange ghostly glow appeared as a distant Very light was fired, and made for them a near dark horizon of tumbled shell-tormented parapet. The trench swerved, and Hanley dimly made out the shape of three crosses – Canadians. Halfway. Fifty yards farther on was another turn, where a piece of corrugated iron revetment had been flung on to the top of the high parapet, where its jagged outline looked like a grotesque heraldic dragon.

It had been an ideal night for gas and would be an ideal dawn – heavy, windless, foggy – for a surprise attack. Hanley had been up and about the trenches most of the night. Since that rotten gas attack on the Somme, where he lost twenty-three men, he took no risks. Up and down the trenches, warning the N.C.O.s to look out for gas. Now he was on the way to his advance posts. Be there in case of an attack. . . .

Splash, squelch, splodge. Somebody coming towards them.

'Who are you?'

'Mockery.'

'Is that the word tonight, Parker?'

'Yessir.'

'That you, Hanley?' Voice coming towards them.

'Hullo, Williams. I thought you were in Hurdle Alley?'

'I was, but I thought I'd have a look at these posts. They're a hell of a way from the front line.'

'I know. Damn this organization in depth. Are they all right?'

'Yes. He sent over about forty minnies, Ser'ant Cramp said, but no casualties. He was flipping over some of those flying pineapples when I left.'

From their own back areas came an irregular but ceaseless crashing of artillery. Heavy shells shrilled high above them as they swooped at enemy communications and night parties.

'Strafing the old Boche a good bit tonight,' said Williams.

'Yes, it's been quite heavy. Might almost be a windup at H.Q.'

'Boche are very quiet tonight.'

'Yes; well, cheerio. Tell Thompson to keep our breakfast hot; and don't stand down until I get back.'

'Right you are, cheerio.'

Hanley visited his posts. They were established in a ruined and unrepaired German trench at the foot of a long forward slope. This had once been the British front line, but was now held only by scattered observation posts, with the main front line several hundred yards to the rear. The British bombardment increased, and the shrill scream of the passing shells was almost continuous. Very lights and rockets went up from the German lines. Hanley cursed the loss of his torch – damned difficult to get about without it. He came to the first post.

'You there, Ser'ant Tomlinson?'

A figure moved in the darkness.

'Yes, sir.'

'Anything to report?'

'No, sir.'

'Mr. Williams said there were some minnies and pineapples.'

'Yes, sir, but it's very quiet, sir.'

'Um. Any patrols still out?'

'No, sir, all in.'

'Very well. Carry on, ser'ant.'

'Very good, sir.'

Much the same news at the other posts. Hanley returned to Number 1 post, nearest the communication trench, at dawn. The men were standing to. Hanley got on the fire-step in a shell-smashed abandoned bay, and watched with his glasses slung round his neck. The artillery had died down to a couple of batteries, when the first perceptible lightening of the air came. Hanley felt cold in his mud-soaked breeches and tunic. Very gradually, very slowly, the darkness dissipated, as if thin imperceptible veils were being rolled up in a transformation scene. The British wire became visible. In the trembling misty light No Man's Land seemed alive with strange shapes and movements. Hanley pressed cold hands on his hot eyes, puffy with lack of sleep. He looked again. Yes, yes, surely, they were climbing over the parapet and lying down in front. He seized a rifle leaning against the trench, loaded with an S.O.S. rocket bomb. Funny Sergeant Tomlinson and the men were so silent. Perhaps he was imagining things, the same old dawn-mirage movement which had been responsible for so many false alarms. He waited a couple of minutes with closed eyes, and then looked very carefully through his glasses. Silly ass! The men coming over the parapets were the German wire pickets. He put the rifle down, glad the men had not seen him, and went round the traverse to Sergeant Tomlinson and Parker.

'Stand to for another twenty minutes, ser'ant, and then let two men from Number 2 post and two from Number 4 go and get your breakfasts.'

'Very good, sir.'

On the way back Hanley found his torch – the glass bulb was smashed; like most things in this bloody war, he reflected. Well, they'd passed another dawn without an attack – that was something. He got on a fire-step in the main line and took another look. A cloudy but rainless morning. Not a sign of life in the enemy trenches, scarcely a sound. He gave the order to stand down, and sent Parker to join his section for breakfast.

The company dug-out was a large one, built as the headquarters of a German battalion. It was remarkably lousy. Hanley threw his torch, revolver-belt, and helmet on his wire and sacking bed, and sat down on a box beside a small table laid with four knives and forks on a newspaper. He felt tired, too tired even to enjoy the hot bacon and eggs which formed the infantry officers' best meal of the day. The three subalterns chatted. Hanley pushed away his plate and stood up.

'I'm going to turn in. Tell the signaller to wake me if anything important happens.'

'Right-o.'

Hanley hung up his revolver and helmet, arranged his pack as a pillow, swung himself still booted and wet on to the bed, and wrapped himself in a blanket. For a few minutes he lay drowsily, listening to the throb of blood in his head and the quiet mutter of the other officers. His eyes still ached even when shut. He drowsed, then half awoke as he remembered that he had not indented for enough ammunition, decided that could wait, and – was dead asleep.

Hanley opened his eyes and lay quite still. Why were they talking so loudly? In a flash he was wide awake and swung up, sitting with his legs over the side of the bed. The colonel. Damn! Being found asleep like that! And, of course, the colonel would not know that he had been up and down the line all night. Damn! Well, never mind. He gave one dab with both hands at his rumpled hair, and stood up.

'Good morning, sir.'

'Oh, good morning, Hanley. Williams said you'd been up all night. Sorry to disturb you.'

'Quite all right, sir.'

A large-scale trench map of their sector was spread on the table, half concealing another smaller-scale artillery map of the whole district.

'Just sit down for a few minutes, Hanley. I've got important news.'

The other officers grouped beside them, gazing at the colonel and listening.

'Very important news,' the colonel went on in a slow voice, 'and not particularly pleasant, I'm afraid.'

He pulled a neat bundle of documents from his pocket, opened one labelled 'SECRET AND CONFIDENTIAL' and spread it on the table. They all gazed at it – the inexorable decree of Fate – and then again at the colonel, the agent of that Fate, of all their fates.

'That is a confidential document from Corps Headquarters. I'll tell you briefly what it is, and you can look it over afterwards. The night before last the division on our left made an identification raid, and captured a prisoner. From this and other information it seems certain that we shall be attacked – tomorrow morning – about an hour before dawn.'

Each of the four company officers drew a short imperceptible breath, glanced at each other and then quickly away. Hanley leaned his elbow on the table.

'Yes, sir?'

'It will be a surprise attack, with a very short but violent preliminary bombardment.' The colonel spoke very slowly and deliberately, looking down absently at the map, and gently twisting the lowest button of his tunic with the fingers of his right hand. 'All reports confirm our information, and the Air Force report great enemy activity behind the lines. You heard the bombardment of their communications last night.'

'Yes, sir.'

There was complete silence in the dug-out, as the colonel paused. A pile of tin plates fell with a clatter in the servants' compartment. None of the officers moved. Hanley noticed how clean the colonel's gas bag was.

'There will probably be twenty to thirty German divisions in the attack, which will be on a sixteen-mile front. We are about in the middle.'

'Yes, sir.'

The colonel moved on his box. He stretched out all the fingers of his left hand, and tapped rapidly on the table alternately with the stretched little finger and thumb.

'The Canadian Corps and several reserve divisions are being brought up at once to occupy a position about five miles to our rear. They cannot fully man the whole battle line before three tomorrow afternoon. Our duty is to delay the enemy advance until that time or longer. Our positions must be held at all costs, to the last man.'

There was a long silence. The colonel ceased drumming with his fingers and looked at them.

'Have you any questions to ask?'

'Yes, sir. Am I to leave my posts out?'

'Two hours before dawn, you will withdraw them to strengthen your own line. One section, with a sergeant and a subaltern, will remain at the end of the communication trench. The subaltern will be a volunteer. His duty is to fire a green light when the German attacking line reaches him. The artillery barrage will then shorten to defend your line. You, Hanley, will have a Very-light pistol loaded with a red light, and you will fire it when the first German jumps into your trench. The object, of course, is to inform the artillery when they must shorten the defensive barrage.'

'Yes, sir.'

'Any more questions?'

'No, sir, not for the moment.'

'You'll arrange with your officers, Hanley, as to which shall volunteer to fire the green light.'

'Very good, sir.'

'And I want you to come to a conference of company officers with the brigadier at Battalion Headquarters this afternoon.'

'Very good, sir. What time?'

'Oh, make it three o'clock.'

'Very well, sir.'

The colonel rose.

'You know your battle positions, of course; but we'll discuss that this afternoon. Oh, by the bye, I'm sending up green envelopes for everyone in the company this morning. The letters must be sent down by runner at four. Of course, not a word about the attack must be mentioned either to N.C.O.s or men until after the letters have gone.'

'Of course, sir.'

'And – er – naturally you will not mention the matter yourselves.'

'No, sir, of course not.'

'All right. Good-bye. Will you come along with me, Hanley? I should like to walk round your main defence line with you.'

'Very good, sir.'

There was silence in the dug-out. They could hear the colonel and Hanley scuffling up the low dug-out stairs. Williams tapped a cigarette on his case and bent down to light it at the candle burning on the table. He puffed a mouthful of smoke, with a twist to his lips.

'Well, that's that. Napoo, eh?'

'Looks like it.'

'What about a drink?'

'Right-o.'

Williams shouted:

'Thomp-sooon.'

From the distance came a muffled: 'Sir?'

A Tommy appeared in the doorway.

'Bring us a bottle of whisky and the mugs.'

'Very good, sir.'

All that day Hanley was in a state of dazed hebetude, from which he emerged from time to time. He felt vaguely surprised that everything was so much as usual. There were sentries at their posts, runners going along the trenches, an occasional airplane overhead, a little artillery – just the ordinary routine of trench warfare. And yet within twenty-four hours their trenches would be obliterated, he and thousands with him would be dead, obliterated, unless by some chance, some odd freak, he was made prisoner. He heard repeated over and over again in his head the words: 'Position must be held at all costs, position must be held at all costs.' He felt suddenly angry. Held at all costs! All jolly fine and large to write from the safety of Montreuil, but what about those who had to make good such dramatic sentiments with their lives? The front was ridiculously denuded of men – why, his own under-strength company held very nearly a battalion front, and had a flank to guard as well. If they fought like madmen and stood to the last man, they might hold up three waves – an hour at most. And they were asked to hold out for nearly twelve hours! Ridiculous, good God, ridiculous!

He found the colonel shaking him by the arm.

'What's the matter with you, Hanley? You don't seem to hear what I'm saying.'

'I beg your pardon, sir. I . . .'

'I think you ought to bring a Lewis gun up to this point. You've got an excellent field of fire here.'

'Very good, sir.'

Hanley noted the change to be made in his field service message book. They walked on, and the colonel made various other suggestions – so many orders – which Hanley duly noted. The colonel paused at the corner of the communication trench leading to Battalion Headquarters. He waved to the orderlies to stand apart.

'We'll discuss the general plan of defence at the conference this afternoon. Make a note of anything that occurs to you, any information you want, and bring it up.'

'Right, sir.'

The colonel hesitated a moment.

'It's a very difficult position, Hanley, I know, but we must all do our duty.'

'Of course, sir.'

'I shall lead the counter-attack of the Reserve Company myself.'

'Yes, sir.'

'A great deal depends on our putting up a good show.'

'Yes, sir.'

'I suggest you go round to the dug-out and speak to all your men this evening. Put a good face on it, you know. Tell them we are all prepared, and shall easily beat off the attack, and that reinforcements are being hurried up to relieve us. And above all impress upon them that these trenches *must* be held at all costs.'

'Very good, sir.'

The colonel held out his hand.

'I may not have another opportunity to speak to you in private. Good-bye, and the best of luck. I know you'll do your duty.'

'Thank you, sir. Good-bye.'

'Good-bye.'

When Hanley stooped under the low entrance of the dug-out chamber, the three subalterns were seated round the table with flushed cheeks, talking loudly. The whisky bottle was more than half-empty. A sudden spurt of anger shot through him. He strode up to the table and knocked the cork level with the top of the bottle neck with one hard smack of his hand. He spoke harshly:

'What's this nonsense?'

Williams, the eldest of the three subalterns, answered, half-defiantly, half-ashamedly:

'We're only having a drink. Where's the harm?'

'Only a drink! Before lunch! Now, look here, you fellows. The whisky that's left in that bottle is all that's going to be drunk in this mess between now and dawn tomorrow. Understand? One of the damned stupidities of this damned war is that every officer thinks it's the thing to be a boozer. It isn't. The men don't drink. They get a tablespoon of rum a day. Why should we make sots of ourselves? We're responsible for their lives. See? And we're responsible for these trenches. We've got to leave 'em on stretchers or stay here and manure 'em. See? We've got a bloody rotten job ahead of us, a stinking rotten job, and I wish those who ordered it were here to carry out their own damned orders. But they're not. Not bloody likely. But the people at home trust us. We're responsible to them, first and foremost. We took on the job, and we've got to carry it out. And carry it out dead bloody sober. Got me?'

The men were silent, looking sheepishly at the newspaper on the table with its wet rings from mug bottoms. Hanley took an empty mug and tossed some of the whisky from Williams' mug into it.

'Drink up. Here's hell!'

They drank.

Hanley shouted:

'Thomp-soooon!'

Thompson appeared in the door.

'Take those mugs away.'

'Very good, sir.'

'How many bottles of whisky have you?'

'Three, sir.'

'Bring them here, and a sandbag.'

'Very good, sir.'

Hanley scribbled a few words in his message book, and tore out the slip. He put the bottles in the sandbag.

'Parker!'

Parker in his turn appeared.

'Sir?'

'Take that sandbag down to Battalion H.Q. Give it to one of the officers, and bring back his signed receipt.'

'Very good, sir.'

The other officers exchanged glances. Williams, who had his back turned to Hanley, made a grimace of derision. The others frowned at him.

Hanley was busy throughout the day, making arrangements, giving orders, attending the conference – which lasted a long time – and going round to speak to the men. He only had time to write a very brief letter to his wife, enclosing one still briefer for his father. He wrote calmly, almost coldly in his effort to avoid emotion and self-pity. He even managed to squeeze out a joke for each letter. As soon as they were finished the two letters vanished in the open sandbag containing the company mail, and the runner started at once for Headquarters. Somehow it was a relief to have those letters gone. The last links with England, with life, were broken. Finished, done with, almost forgotten. It was easier to carry on now.

But was it? There was that damned business of the volunteer subaltern. Hanley rubbed his clenched fist against his cheek, and found that he had forgotten to shave. He called his servant and told him to bring some hot water in a cigarette tin. Shaving for the last time. Hardly worth it, really. Still, must be done. Morale, and all that.

He shaved carefully. One of the subalterns went out to relieve the officer on duty. One was asleep. Williams was writing a situation report. Hanley bit the back of his hand hard, then shoved both hands in his breeches pockets, looking at Williams' bent head.

'Williams!'

Williams looked up.

'Yes?'

'There's this business of the volunteer to – '

'Oh, that's all settled.'

'Settled!'

'Yes. I'm going.'

'You're going! But you've only been married two months.'

'Yes. That's why I thought I'd like to get it over as quickly as possible.'

'But I was going to put your platoon at the end of Hurdle Alley. You might just be able to get back to battalion, you know.'

'And feel a swine for the rest of my life – which would be about two hours? Thanks. No, I'd rather get it over, if you don't mind, Hanley.'

'Oh, all right.'

They were silent. Then Hanley said:

'Well, I'll just go and talk to the men . . . er . . . So long.'

'So long.'

All working parties were cancelled to give the men as much rest as possible, but there was inevitably a lot of extra work, bringing up ammunition, rations, and water. As soon as dusk fell the whole Reserve Company and some pioneers came up to strengthen the wire. The British artillery was ceaselessly active. Hardly a shot came from the German lines – an ominous sign.

After dinner Hanley lay down to sleep for a few hours. Must be as fresh as possible. He wrapped the blanket up to his chin and shut his eyes. The other three off duty were lying down, too. But Hanley could not sleep. It was all so strange, so strange, and yet so ordinary. Just like any other night, and yet the last night. Inevitably the last night? How could they escape, with orders to hold on at all costs? Half of them would go in the bombardment, which would be terrific. Bombs, bullets, and bayonets would finish off the rest. The dug-outs would be wrecked with bombs and high explosive charges. A few of the wounded might be picked up later. A few of the men might escape down Hurdle Alley after the officers were gone. But no, the N.C.O.s could be relied on to hold out to the last. They were done for, napoo. No *après la guerre* for *them* – *bon soir,* toodle-oo, good-byeeee. The silly words repeated and repeated in his brain until he hated them. He opened his eyes and gazed at the familiar dug-out. His wire bed was at an angle to the others, and he could see the shapes of Williams and the two other officers muffled up silent in their blankets – as still and silent as they would be in twenty-four hours' time. There was the candle burning in the holder roughly bent from a tin biscuit box. The flame was absolutely steady in the airless, earthy smelling dug-out. There were the boxes for seats, the table with its maps, tins of cigarettes, chits, and the five mugs beside the whisky bottle for the last parting drink. The bare, murky walls of chalk were damp and clammy-looking with condensed breath. The revolvers, helmets, and gas bags were hung at the bed-heads. He listened to the other men breathing, and felt an absurd regret at leaving the dug-out to be smashed. After all, that and other dug-outs like it were the only home they had known for months and months. Breaking up the happy home! He became aware that he felt a bit sickish, that he had been feeling like that for several hours, and pretending not to.

He gently drew his wrist from under the blanket and looked at his luminous watch. Eleven thirty-five. He had to be up at two – must get some sleep. With almost a start he noticed that Williams was looking at his own watch in the same stealthy way. So he couldn't sleep either. Poor devil. Profoundly, almost insanely in love with that wife of his. Poor devil. But still, for the matter of that, so was Hanley in love with his wife. His heart seemed to turn in his body, and he felt an acute pain in the muscles above it as he suddenly realized fully that it was all over, that he would never see her again, never feel her mouth pressed to his, never again touch her lovely, friendly body. He clutched his hand over his face until it hurt to prevent himself from groaning. God, what bloody agony! O God, he'd be a mass of dead rotting decay, and she'd still be young and beautiful and alert and desirable, O God, and her life would run on, run on, there'd be all the grief and the sorrowing for her and tears in a cold widowed bed, O God, but the years would run on and she'd still be young and desirable, and somebody else would want her, some youngster, some wangler, and youth and her flesh and life would be clamorous, and her bed would no longer be cold and widowed. O God, God. Something wet ran down his cheek. Not a tear, but the cold clammy sweat from his forehead. God, what agony!

Hanley suddenly sat up. If he was suffering like that, Williams must be suffering, too. Better to get up and pretend to talk than lie and agonize like that. He got out of bed. Williams raised his head:

'What's up. It isn't two, is it?'

The other men looked up, too, showing that neither of them had been asleep. Hanley shivered and rubbed his hands to warm them in the chill dug-out.

'No, only five to twelve. But I couldn't sleep. Hope I don't disturb you. Benson must be relieved in a few minutes,' he added inconsequently.

The other three rolled out of bed and stood stretching and rubbing their hands.

'Too cold to sleep in this damned damp place,' said one of them.

'What about a drink?'

'If you have it now, you can't have it later on,' said Hanley. 'Better wait until two.'

Williams put on his equipment and helmet and went up to relieve Benson. The others sat on the boxes trying to talk. Benson came down.

'Anything on?' asked Hanley casually.

'Lots of lights, ordinary strafing on their side. A hell of a bombardment from our side.'

'Perhaps if they see we've got wind of it, they'll postpone the attack?' suggested the youngest officer.

'Rot,' said Benson. 'They know jolly well that all this part of the line has been denuded to feed the Fifth Army. They'll attack, all right.'

They were silent. Hanley looked at his watch. Five past twelve. How damnably slowly the time went; and yet these were their last minutes on earth. He felt something had to be done.

'Let's have a hand at bridge.'

'What, tonight, now?'

'Well, why not? It's no good sitting here grumping like owls, and you don't suggest a prayer meeting, do you?'

The last suggestion was met with oaths of a forcible nature. Hanley cleared the table and threw down the cards.

'Cut for deal.'

Just before two, Hanley slipped into his breeches pocket the ten francs he had won, and stood up. He put on trench coat and muffler, tried his broken torch for about the twentieth time, then threw it down disgustedly and fitted on his equipment. The subaltern who was to relieve Williams on trench duty was already dressed and waiting. Hanley put on his hat and turned to the others.

'I'll come round and see you after you've taken up battle positions; but if by any chance I don't see you again – cheerio.'

'Cheerio.'

They found Williams, his runner, and a sergeant waiting in the trench outside the dug-out entrance.

'Anything doing?'

'Nothing particular. I went on patrol. Their wire's got gaps cut, with knife-rests in the gaps, all the way along.'

'Um.'

'Lot of signal rockets, too.'

'I see. Our artillery seems to have ceased altogether.'

'Saving ammunition for the show.'

'Be more sensible to strafe now while the Boche is taking up battle positions.'

'Oh, well, that's the staff's job, not ours.'

Hanley, Williams, the sergeant, two runners, started for the Outpost Line. The trench was drier, the night not so dark, with faint stars mistily gleaming among light clouds. Weather clearing up –

B

just the Boche's luck again. The five men moved along without talking, absorbed partly in a strange anxious preoccupation, partly in keeping upright on the slippery trench. Hanley and Williams, of course, knew the full extent of their danger, had faced the ultimate despair, passed beyond revolt or hope. The sergeant still hoped – that he might be wounded and taken prisoner. The two men only knew they were 'in for a show'. All were dry-mouthed, a little sickish with apprehension, a little awkward in all their movements; the thought of deserting their posts never even occurred to them.

They passed the three Canadian crosses, distinctly outlined on the quiet sky; then the dragon piece of corrugated iron. At the end of the communication trench they found waiting the men from the four posts, under a sergeant. Hanley spoke in low tones – there might be advance patrols lying just outside their wire.

'All your men present, ser'ant?'

'Yes, sir.'

'Right. You know your orders. See that each section joins its own platoon, and then report to your own platoon commander. Don't waste time.'

'Very good, sir.'

The line of men filed past them in the darkness. For the hundredth time Hanley noticed the curious pathos of fatigue in these silent moving figures – the young bodies somehow tired to age and apathy. When they had gone he took Williams a little aside.

'If I were you, I should see that each of you occupies a separate bay. Get in the first bay yourself, then the runner, then the sergeant. They won't dare try to bolt back past you. Besides – er – there's more chance if you're spread out.'

'I was wondering what happens if all three of us are knocked out before the Boche actually gets into the trench, and so no green light is fired?'

'Oh, we must risk that. Besides, there are similar volunteer parties on every company front.'

'I see.'

'I took a compass bearing from the fire-step outside Company H.Q. yesterday, so I shan't miss your light. I expect they'll be on us ten minutes later. Perhaps we'll beat off the first two or three attacks.'

'Yes. Perhaps.'

They were silent. Then Hanley made an effort.

'Well, good-bye, old man. Best of luck.'

'Best of luck, good-bye.'

They were too shy and English even to shake hands.

It was past three when Hanley and Parker got back to their own line and found the whole company standing to in battle positions. Hanley kept his signallers on the first floor of the big dug-out. He sent off to Battalion Headquarters the code message which meant they were in battle positions and all ready. He took a candle and went down to the lower dug-out, where they had spent so many nights. It looked barer and damper than ever, empty except for the bare sacking beds, the boxes, the table.

Outside in the trench the air was moist and fresh. He took two Very pistols, one loaded with green, one with red, and laid them on either side of him on the parapet. Hanley was at the extreme left of the bay, with two riflemen to his right. Twenty yards to his left was the communication trench leading to the outpost line, now blocked with wire and knife-rests, and guarded by a bombing section.

A signaller came up from the dug-out with a message. Hanley went down and read it by the light of a candle. He noticed the bowed back and absorbed look of a signaller tapping out a message on a Fullerphone. The message he had received simply reiterated the order that their positions were to be held at all costs. Hanley felt angry, screwed up the piece of paper and stuffed it in his pocket. Damn them, how many more times did they think that order had to be given? He returned to the trench, and resumed his watch.

3.50 A.M. One battery of German guns languidly firing on back areas – pretence that all was as usual.

3.52 A.M. Signal rockets all along the German line. Then silence.

3.55 A.M. Two miles to his right a fierce bombardment, stretching over several miles. The battle had begun.

3.57 A.M. Two miles to his left another bombardment. The British artillery on their own front opened up a defensive barrage.

4 A.M. With a terrific crash, which immediately blotted out the roar of the other bombardments, the German artillery on their own front came into action. Hanley half-recoiled. He had been in several big bombardments, and thought he had experienced the utmost limit of artillery. But this was more tremendous, more hellish, more appalling than anything he had experienced. The trench of the outpost line was one continuous line of red, crashing trench mortars and shells. The communication trench was plastered with five-nines. Shells were falling all along their own line – he heard the sharp cry 'Stretcher-bearer' very faintly from somewhere close at hand.

The confusion and horror of a great battle descended on him. The crash of shells, the roar of the guns, the brilliant flashes, the eerie piercing scream of a wounded man, the rattle of the machine-guns, the Lewis guns, the two riflemen beside him madly working the bolts of their rifles and fumbling as with trembling hands they thrust in a fresh clip of cartridges – all somehow perceived, but thrust aside in his intense watch. A green light went up about half a mile to the left, then another a little nearer. Hanley stared more intently in the direction of Williams's post – and found himself saying over and over again without knowing he was saying it: 'O God, help him, O God, help him, O God, help him.'

Suddenly two green lights appeared, one fired straight up as a signal – probably Williams – the other almost along the ground, as if fired at somebody – probably the runner, wounded or in a panic. Sergeant dead, no doubt – Williams and his runner dead, too, by now. Hanley fired a green light. Two minutes later the British barrage shortened.

Hanley grasped the Very pistol loaded with red. Their turn now.

'Stretcher-bearer, stretcher-bearer!'

Crash! A shell right on their bay.

Hanley staggered and felt a fearful pain in his right knee where a shell splinter had hit him. In the faint light of dawn he saw vaguely that one of the riflemen lay huddled on the fire-step, leaving his rifle still on the parapet; the other man had been blown backwards into the trench, and lay with his feet grimly and ludicrously caught in a torn piece of revetment. His helmet had been knocked from his head.

Faint pops of bombs to his immediate left – they were coming up the communication trench. He peered into the steel-smashed light of dawn, but saw only smoke and the fierce red flash of explosions.

Suddenly, to his left, he saw German helmets coming up the communication trench – they had passed the wire barrier! He looked to his right – a little knot of Germans had got through the wire – a Lewis gun swept them away like flies. He felt the blood running down his leg.

Somebody was standing beside him. A voice, far off, was speaking:

'Bombing attack beaten off, sir.'

'Very good, carry on.'

'There's only two of us left, sir.'

'Carry on.'

'Very good, sir.'

More Germans on the right; another, longer row coming up the communication trench. Then, suddenly, Germans seemed to spring up in every direction. Hanley fired six shots from his Webley at those in front. He saw others falling hit, or jumping into the trench on either side.

A red light shot up straight in the air. A second later two bombs fell in the bay. A torn, crumpled figure collapsed sideways. The Germans reorganized, while the moppers-up did their job.

From: *Roads to Glory*, by permission of the author.

RICHARD ALDINGTON was born in Hampshire in 1892, and educated at Dover College and London University. Literary editor of an arts magazine *The Egoist* in 1913, he joined up in 1916 at the age of twenty-four as an infantry private, was later commissioned, and served on the Western Front where he was badly gassed, the damage being more or less permanent. After the war he earned a living as a poet, writer, and translator, the bitter war book *Death of a Hero* making his name. Among other books, Aldington wrote a controversial biography of Lawrence of Arabia. He died at his home in France in 1962.

THE KING OF YPRES

John Buchan

Private Peter Galbraith, of the 3rd Lennox Highlanders, awoke with a splitting headache and the consciousness of an intolerable din. At first he thought it was the whistle from the forge, which a year ago had pulled him from his bed when he was a puddler in Motherwell. He scrambled to his feet, and nearly cracked his skull against a low roof. That, and a sound which suggested that the heavens were made of canvas which a giant hand was rending, cleared his wits and recalled him to the disagreeable present. He lit the dottle in his pipe, and began to piece out his whereabouts.

Late the night before, the remnants of his battalion had been brought in from the Gheluvelt trenches to billets in Ypres. That last week he had gone clean off his sleep. He had not been dry for a fortnight, his puttees had rotted away, his greatcoat had disappeared in a mud-hole, and he had had no stomach for what food

A Scots soldier of the 10th Argyll and Sutherland Highlanders.— CAMERA PRESS LTD.

could be got. He had seen half his battalion die before his eyes, and day and night the shells had burst round him till the place looked like the ironworks at Motherwell on a foggy night. The worst of it was that he had never come to grips with the Boches, which he had long decided was the one pleasure left to him in life. He had got far beyond cursing, though he had once had a talent that way. His mind was as sodden as his body, and his thoughts had been focussed on the penetrating power of a bayonet when directed against a plump Teutonic chest. There had been a German barber in Motherwell called Schultz, and he imagined the enemy as a million Schultzes – large, round men who talked with the back of their throat.

In billets he had scraped off the worst part of the mud, and drunk half a bottle of wine which a woman had given him. It tasted like red ink, but anything liquid was better than food. Sleep was what he longed for, but he could not get it. The Boches were shelling the town, and the room he shared with six others seemed as noisy as the Gallowgate on a Saturday night. He wanted to get deep down into the earth where there was no sound; so, while the others snored, he started out to look for a cellar. In the black darkness, while the house rocked to the shell reverberations, he had groped his way down the stairs, found a door which led to another flight, and, slipping and stumbling, had come to a narrow, stuffy chamber which smelt of potatoes. There he had lain down on some sacks and fallen into a frowsty slumber.

His head was spinning, but the hours of sleep had done him good. He felt a slight appetite for breakfast, as well as an intolerable thirst. He groped his way up the stairs, and came out in a dilapidated hall lit by a dim November morning.

There was no sign of the packs which had been stacked there the night before. He looked for a Boche's helmet which he had brought in as a souvenir, but that was gone. Then he found the room where he had been billeted. It was empty, and only the stale smell of tobacco told of its occupants.

Lonely, disconsolate, and oppressed with thoughts of future punishment, he moved towards the street door. Suddenly the door of a side room opened and a man came out, a furtive figure, with a large, pasty face. His pockets bulged, and in one hand was a silver candlestick. At the sight of Galbraith he jumped back and held up a pistol.

'Pit it down, man, and tell's what's come ower this place?' said the soldier. For answer, a bullet sang past his ear and shivered a plaster Venus.

Galbraith gave his enemy the butt of his rifle and laid him out. From his pockets he shook out a mixed collection of loot. He took possession of his pistol, and kicked him with some vehemence into a cupboard.

'That yin's a thief,' was his spoken reflection. 'There's something michty wrong wi' Wipers the day.'

His head was clearing, and he was getting very wroth. His battalion had gone off and left him in a cellar, and miscreants were abroad. It was time for a respectable man to be up and doing. Besides, he wanted his breakfast. He fixed his bayonet, put the pistol in his pocket, and emerged into the November drizzle.

The streets suddenly were curiously still. The occasional shell-fire came to his ears as if through layers of cotton-wool. He put this down to dizziness from lack of food, and made his way to what looked like an *estaminet*. The place was full of riotous people who were helping themselves to drinks, while a distracted landlord wrung his hands. He flew to Galbraith, the tears running down his cheeks, and implored him in broken words.

'Vere ze Engleesh?' he cried. 'Ze méchants rob me. Zere is une émeute. Vere ze officers?'

'That's what I'm wantin' to ken mysel',' said Galbraith.

'Zey are gone,' wailed the innkeeper. 'Zere is no gendarme or anyzing, and I am rob.'

'Where's the polis? Get the Provost, man. D'ye tell me there's no polis left?'

'I am rob,' the wail continued. 'Ze méchants rob ze magasins and ve vill be assassinés.'

Light was dawning upon Private Galbraith. The British troops had left Ypres for some reason which he could not fathom, and there was no law or order in the little city. At other times he had hated the law as much as any man, and his relations with the police had often been strained. Now he realized that he had done them an injustice. Disorder suddenly seemed to him the one thing intolerable. Here had he been undergoing a stiff discipline for weeks, and if that was his fate no civilian should be allowed on the loose. He was a British soldier – marooned here by no fault of his own – and it was his business to keep up the end of the British Army and impose the King's peace upon the unruly. His temper was getting hot, but he was curiously happy.

He marched into the *estaminet*. 'Oot o' here, ye scum!' he bellowed. 'Sortez, ye cochons!'

The revellers were silent before the apparition. Then one, drunker than the rest, flung a bottle which grazed his right ear. That put the finishing touch to his temper. Roaring like a bull, he was among them, prodding their hinder parts with his bayonet, and now and then reversing his rifle to crack a head. He had not played centre-forward in the old days at Celtic Park for nothing. The place emptied in a twinkling – all but one man whose legs could not support him. Him Private Galbraith seized by the scruff and the slack of his trousers, and tossed into the street.

'Now I'll hae my breakfast,' he said to the trembling landlord.

Private Galbraith, much the better for his exercise, made a hearty meal of bread and cold ham, and quenched his thirst with two bottles of Hazebrouck beer. He had also a little brandy, and pocketed the flask, for which the landlord refused all payment. Then, feeling a giant refreshed, he sallied into the street.

'I'm off to look for your Provost,' he said. 'If ye have ony mair trouble, ye'll find me at the Toun Hall.'

A shell had plumped into the middle of the causeway, and the place was empty. Private Galbraith, despising shells, swaggered up the open, his disreputable kilt swinging about his putteeless legs, the remnant of a bonnet set well on the side of his shaggy red head, and the light of battle in his eyes. For once he was arrayed on the side of the angels, and the thought encouraged him mightily. The brandy had fired his imagination.

Adventure faced him at the next corner. A woman was struggling with two men – a slim pale girl with dark hair. No sound came from her lips, but her eyes were bright with terror. Galbraith started to run, shouting sound British oaths. The men let the woman go, and turned to face him. One had a pistol, and for the second time that day a bullet just missed its mark. An instant later a clean bayonet thrust had ended the mortal career of the marksman, and the other had taken to his heels.

'I'll learn thae lads to be sae free wi' their popguns,' said the irate soldier. 'Haud up, Mem. It's a' by wi' noo. Losh! The wumman's fentit!'

Private Galbraith was as shy of women as of his Commanding Officer, and he had not bargained for this duty. She was clearly a lady from her dress and appearance, and this did not make it easier. He supported her manfully, addressing to her the kind of encouragements which a groom gives to a horse. 'Canny now, Mem. Haud up! Ye've no cause to be feared.'

Then he remembered the brandy in his pocket, and with much awkwardness managed to force some drops between her lips. To his vast relief she began to come to. Her eyes opened and stared uncomprehendingly at her preserver. Then she found her voice.

'Thank God, the British have come back!' she said in excellent English.

'No, Mem; not yet. It's just me, Private Galbraith, "C" Company, 3rd Battalion, Lennox Highlanders. Ye keep some bad lots in this toun.'

'Alas, what can we do? The place is full of spies, and they will stir up the dregs of the people and make Ypres a hell. Oh, why did the British go? Our good men are all with the army, and there are only old folks and wastrels left.'

'Rely upon me, Mem,' said Galbraith stoutly. 'I was just settin' off to find your Provost.'

She puzzled at the word, and then understood.

'He has gone!' she cried. 'The Maire went to Dunkirk a week ago, and there is no authority in Ypres.'

'Then we'll make yin. Here's the minister. We'll speir at him.'

An old priest, with a lean, grave face, had come up.

'Ah, Mam'selle Omèrine,' he cried, 'the devil in our city is unchained. Who is this soldier?'

The two talked in French, while Galbraith whistled and looked at the sky. A shrapnel shell was bursting behind the cathedral, making a splash of colour in the November fog. Then the priest spoke in careful and constrained English.

'There is yet a chance for a strong man. But he must be very strong. Mam'selle will summon her father, Monsieur le Procureur, and we will meet at the Mairie. I will guide you there, *mon brave*.'

The Grande Place was deserted, and in the middle there was a new gaping shell-hole. At the door of a great building, which Galbraith assumed to be the Town Hall, a feeble old porter was struggling with a man. Galbraith scragged the latter and pitched him into the shell-hole. There was a riot going on in a café on the far side which he itched to have a hand in, but he postponed that pleasure to a more convenient season.

Twenty minutes later, in a noble room with frescoed and tapestried walls, there was a strange conference. The priest was there, and Galbraith, and Mam'selle Omèrine, and her father, M. St. Marais. There was a doctor too, and three elderly citizens, and an old warrior who had left an arm on the Yser. Galbraith took charge, with Mam'selle as his interpreter, and in half an hour had constituted a Committee of Public Safety. He had nervous folk to deal with.

'The Germans may enter at any moment, and then we will all be hanged,' said one.

'Nae doot,' said Galbraith; 'but ye needna get your throats cut afore they come.'

'The city is full of the ill-disposed,' said another. 'The Boches have their spies in every alley. We who are so few cannot control them.'

'If it's spies,' said Galbraith firmly, 'I'll take on the job my lone. D'ye think a terrier dowg's feared of a wheen rottens?'*

In the end he had his way, with Mam'selle's help, and had put some confidence into civic breasts. It took him the best part of the

* rats.

afternoon to collect his posse. He got every wounded Belgian that had the use of his legs, some well-grown boys, one or two ancients, and several dozen robust women. There was no lack of weapons, and he armed the lot with a strange collection of French and English rifles, giving pistols to the section leaders. With the help of the Procureur, he divided the city into beats and gave his followers instructions. They were drastic orders, for the situation craved for violence.

He spent the evening of his life. So far as he remembered afterwards, he was in seventeen different scraps. Strayed revellers were leniently dealt with – the canal was a cooling experience. Looters were rounded up, and, if they showed fight, summarily disposed of. One band of bullies made a stout resistance, killed two of his guards, and lost half a dozen dead. He got a black eye, a pistol-bullet through his sleeve, a wipe on the cheek from a carving-knife, and he lost the remnants of his bonnet. Fifty-two prisoners spent the night in the cellars of the Mairie.

About midnight he found himself in the tapestried chamber. 'We'll hae to get a Proclamation,' he had announced; 'a gude strong yin, for we maun conduct this job according to the rules.' So the Procureur had a document drawn up bidding all inhabitants of Ypres keep indoors except between the hours of 10 A.M. and noon, and 3 and 5 P.M.; forbidding the sale of alcohol in all forms; and making theft and violence and the carrying of arms punishable by death. There was a host of other provisions which Galbraith imperfectly understood, but when the thing was translated to him he approved its spirit. He signed the document in his large sprawling hand – 'Peter Galbraith, 1473, Pte., 3rd Lennox Highlanders, Acting Provost of Wipers.'

'Get that prentit,' he said, 'and pit up copies at every street corner and on a' the public-hooses. And see that the doors o' the publics are boardit up. That'll do for the day. I'm feelin' verra like my bed.'

Mam'selle Omèrine watched him with a smile. She caught his eye and dropped him a curtsey.

'Monsieur le Roi d'Ypres,' she said.

He blushed hotly.

For the next few days Private Galbraith worked harder than ever before in his existence. For the first time he knew responsibility, and that toil which brings honour with it. He tasted the sweets of office; and he, whose aim in life had been to scrape through with the minimum of exertion, now found himself the inspirer of the maximum in others.

At first he scorned advice, being shy and nervous. Gradually, as he felt his feet, he became glad of other people's wisdom. Especially he leaned on two, Mam'selle Omèrine and her father. Likewise the priest, whom he called the minister.

By the second day the order in Ypres was remarkable. By the third day it was phenomenal; and by the fourth a tyranny. The little city for the first time for seven hundred years fell under the sway of a despot. A citizen had to be on his best behaviour, for the Acting Provost's eye was on him. Never was seen so sober a place. Three permits for alcohol and no more were issued, and then only on the plea of medical necessity. Peter handed over to the doctor the flask of brandy he had carried off from the *estaminet* – Provosts must set an example.

The Draconian code promulgated the first night was not adhered to. Looters and violent fellows went to gaol instead of the gallows. But three spies were taken and shot after a full trial. That trial was the master effort of Private Galbraith – based on his own regimental experience and memories of a Sheriff Court in Lanarkshire, where he had twice appeared for poaching. He was extraordinarily punctilious about forms, and the three criminals – their guilt was clear, and they were the scum of creation – had something more than justice. The Acting Provost pronounced sentence, which the priest translated, and a file of *mutilés* in the yard did the rest.

'If the Boches get in here we'll pay for this day's work,' said the judge cheerfully; 'but I'll gang easier to the grave for havin' got rid o' thae swine.'

On the fourth day he had a sudden sense of dignity. He examined his apparel, and found it very bad. He needed a new bonnet, a new kilt, and puttees, and he would be the better of a new shirt. Being aware that commandeering for personal use ill suited with his office, he put the case before the Procureur, and a *Commission de Ravitaillement* was appointed. Shirts and puttees were easily got, but the kilt and bonnet were difficulties. But next morning Mam'selle Omèrine brought a gift. It was a bonnet with such a dicing round the rim as no Jock ever wore, and a skirt – it is the truest word – of that pattern which graces the persons of small girls in France. It was not the Lennox tartan, it was not any kind of tartan, but Private Galbraith did not laugh. He accepted the garments with a stammer of thanks – 'They're awfu' braw, and I'm much obliged, Mem' – and, what is more, he put them on. The Ypriotes saw his splendour with approval. It was a proof of his new frame of mind that he did not even trouble to reflect what his comrades would think of his costume, and that he kissed the bonnet affectionately before he went to bed.

That night he had evil dreams. He suddenly saw the upshot of it all – himself degraded and shot as a deserter, and his brief glory pricked like a bubble. Grim forebodings of court-martials assailed him. What would Mam'selle think of him when he was led away in disgrace – he who for a little had been a king? He walked about the floor in a frenzy of disquiet, and stood long at the window peering over the Place, lit by a sudden blink of moonlight. It could never be, he decided. Something desperate would happen first. The crash of a shell a quarter of a mile off reminding him that he was in the midst of war – war with all its chances of cutting knots.

Next morning no Procureur appeared. Then came the priest with a sad face and a sadder tale. Mam'selle had been out late the night before on an errand of mercy, and a shell, crashing through a gable, had sent an avalanche of masonry into the street. She was dead, without pain, said the priest, and in the sure hope of Heaven.

The others wept, but Private Galbraith strode from the room, and in a very little time was at the house of the Procureur. He saw his little colleague laid out for death after the fashion of her Church, and his head suddenly grew very clear and his heart hotter than fire.

'I maun resign this job,' he told the Committee of Public Safety.

'I've been forgettin' that I'm a sodger and no a Provost. It's my duty to get a nick at thae Boches.'

They tried to dissuade him, but he was adamant. His rule was over, and he was going back to serve.

But he was not allowed to resign. For that afternoon, after a week's absence, the British troops came again into Ypres.

They found a decorous little city, and many people who spoke of 'le Roi' – which they assumed to signify the good King Albert. Also, in a corner of the cathedral yard, sitting disconsolately on the edge of a fallen monument, Company Sergeant-Major Macvittie of the 3rd Lennox Highlanders found Private Peter Galbraith.

'Ma God, Galbraith, ye've done it this time! *You'll* catch it in the neck! Absent for a week wi'out leave, and gettin' yoursel' up to look like Harry Lauder! You come along wi' me!'

'I'll come quiet,' said Galbraith with strange meekness. He was wondering how to spell Omèrine St. Marais in case he wanted to write it in his Bible.

The events of the next week were confusing to a plain man. Galbraith was very silent, and made no reply to the chaff with which at first he was greeted. Soon his fellows forbore to chaff him, regarding him as a doomed man who had come well within the pale of the ultimate penalties.

He was examined by his Commanding Officer, and interviewed by still more exalted personages. The story he told was so bare as to be unintelligible. He asked for no mercy, and gave no explanations. But there were other witnesses besides him – the priest, for example, and Monsieur St. Marais, in a sober suit of black and very dark under the eyes.

By and by the Court gave its verdict. Private Peter Galbraith was found guilty of riding roughshod over the King's Regulations; he had absented himself from his battalion without permission; he had neglected his own duties and usurped without authority a number of superior functions; he had been the cause of the death or maltreatment of various persons who, whatever their moral deficiencies, must be regarded for the purposes of the case as civilian Allies. The Court, however, taking into consideration the exceptional circumstances in which Private Galbraith had been placed, inflicted no penalty and summarily discharged the prisoner.

Privately, his Commanding Officer and the still more exalted personages shook hands with him, and told him that he was a devilish good fellow and a credit to the British Army.

But Peter Galbraith cared for none of these things. As he sat again in the trenches at St. Eloi in six inches of water and a foot of mud, he asked his neighbour how many Germans were opposite them.

'I was hearin' that there was maybe fifty thoosand,' was the answer.

Private Galbraith was content. He thought that the whole fifty thousand would scarcely atone for the death of one slim, dark-eyed girl.

JOHN BUCHAN, 1st Baron Tweedsmuir, was born in Perth in 1875, and died in February 1940. A Scottish novelist, war historian, lawyer, and diplomat, Buchan was educated at Scottish grammar schools, Glasgow University, and Brasenose College, Oxford. Called to the Bar (Middle Temple) in 1901, he gave up law because of the success of his adventure novels, *Prester John, Greenmantle, The Thirty-nine Steps*, etc. He served as a war correspondent on the Western Front and was later in charge of news and information at G.H.Q.

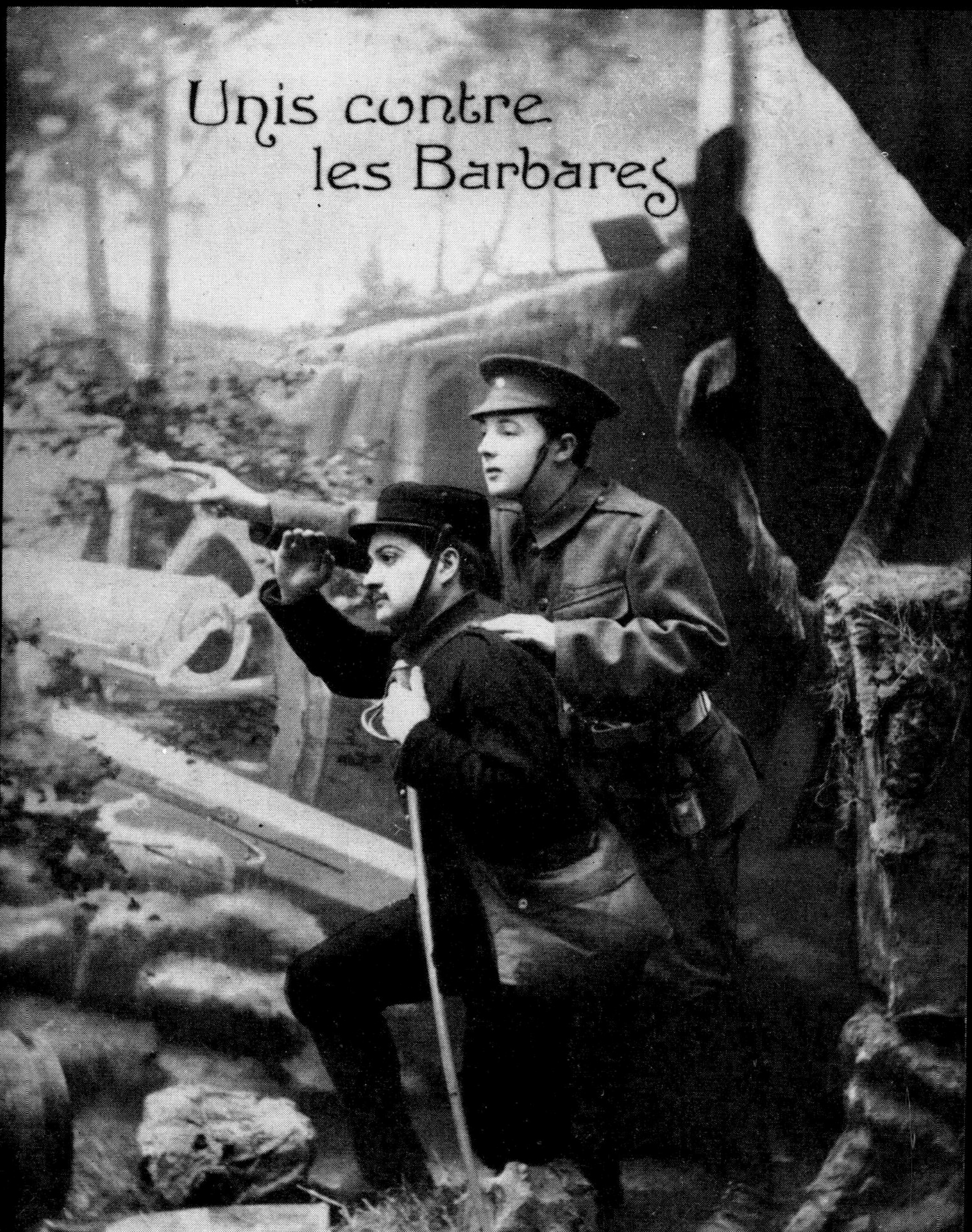
Unis contre
les Barbares

ALL OUR YESTERDAYS
H M Tomlinson

We went through this white town, which was old and sleepy in the early afternoon, and then the road continued till it brought us to ornate iron gates. We drove through them, and over a drawbridge. I did not know who lived there, nor even where it was, but we have to take, on such an occasion, whatever we find within the gates of iron. There my officer abandoned me. Whatever was to follow was for myself alone.

The French house was seen, as I turned a corner of the drive, remote in a diminishing avenue of noble trees. Below the hush of midsummer was the vibration of many wings. The bees were in the limes. I could smell the nectar of that tree; it is full summer when the limes are in flower and the bees get drunk. That was a pleasant confirmation of the season, for the summer to me was doubtful. The house was set deeply in a perspective of rounded foliage, as though

A French postcard of the period, probably taken in late 1914 or early 1915.

I stood in the June of one year, and saw distantly the pale ghost of the old château in a June that was silent, for it was past. I wanted to reach that house, but it seemed as though I could get no nearer to it than the murmuring summer in which I stood. I could only look back to where it was secluded in the silence of a forgotten year.

That was a confusing idea; but then it was a confusing summer, a summer dubious with its immemorial aspect of continuity, yet suggesting bleakly a subtle yet disastrous interruption in the life of the earth; as though common and pleasant things had their accustomed aspect, yet a suspicion had taken us that now we saw only the bright illusion of what was familiar. What had been behind everything was gone. If in one of the arbours of that estate, where stood white statues pensive with ancient secrets they would never disclose, I had surprised a furbelowed lady who ought to have been nowhere but in a picture by Watteau, she might have been more startled than myself. I should have felt that I was the intruder, and should have withdrawn at once from a June which did not belong to me. Not my June; and that was not a lady for me, but only for a gentleman in satin breeches and a brocaded coat. And from one of those arbours, in a vista which was still and suspect, a figure did suddenly emerge. It came out quickly, gave me a direct but not a startled look, and turned towards the château. It had a cockney face, and its khaki dress was unrelieved by ornament except the blue and white armlet of a British signaller. I could see it had no doubt whatever about its year.

I had to believe, after all, that I had not wandered into another age. If I had, others of my own time were lost there with me; or perhaps in a celestial dreaminess the gods had become careless, and had muddled the sunlights and affairs of far different times. For a Sikh, with a rifle that was only a toy in his giant's grasp – a giant with a divided black beard the ends of which were curled up behind his ears – was patrolling the balustrade of a terrace of that French house; below him was a moat in which waterlilies floated. The Indian sentry reached the end of his beat, and paused to look down at the white body of Aphrodite, who stood there with a foot coyly poised over the water she had been about to enter since Louis Soleil was king. War? Not even though a Sikh with fierce whiskers were considering Aphrodite. There was no war. There was only an occasional and inexplicable flutter in the air. The air sometimes shook; the summer day was quite peaceful, but it was not accurately fitted to the earth, it was not quite firm on its base. It gave a sense of insecurity, as though it might be withdrawn from us because it was a mistake, being the misplaced summer of another age and place.

Nor was the interior of the château reassuring. The frail furniture was right, and the ormolu, the crystal candelabra hanging from the painted ceiling, and the tapestries; they were in their place in the serene continuity of pleasant human things. The ladies of the house looked down from the walls out of their frames of heavy gilt, and one of them, a girl of 1779, seemed as surprised as I was to observe soldiers below intent upon typewriters, and the coming and going of British officers.

One of the officers came to me. He knew my name, and met me as if I were one of that household, though I had never seen him before. 'They telephoned from G.H.Q. about you this morning. We were thinking you were lost. The battalion you want is somewhere near Neuve Chapelle, but the ground is rather altered up there since the attack, and it's an unattractive corner. But we've got a guide for you – here he is, too. Lieutenant Jones . . .'

The lieutenant was boyish, and had the brusque candour of shyness. 'I offered to take you before I knew where you wanted to go. Shall we start at once? It's fairly quiet there now, so we'd better get it over.'

We had a brief run by car through an uninhabited country, and then, for no reason that I could see – but perhaps reason was not there – the young soldier hid the car by a hedge, and said we must walk. We took a straight road through an avenue of poplar trees; on each side of it was a stagnant ditch, and peeps over flat meadows. The sun was on it, but if his light had been blue, and so the land had had that sinister complexion of the spectral vista we get through a tinted window, it could not have been more forbidding. It was an earth changed in nature. We were alone in it.

This region was enchanted, without a doubt, but it offered us no clue. Cavities that were raw and deep were frequent in our road. We came to a footbridge, and the ditch there was widened into a circular basin of black slime as smooth and polished as glass; its duckweed and rushes were plastered fanwise across our path, and had stuck to neighbouring walls. The muck was new; the water was still draining from it as ink. We approached a large pool of blood, and separated to walk round it. Its extravagance alarmed me, but, except that my guide must have seen it to have avoided it, he gave no other sign that he admitted its existence. It spread in front of an *estaminet*. The door of the inn was open, and beside the door was a chair; but nobody was in the chair; nobody sat in it contemplating that mystery in the middle of the road. The *estaminet* was deserted. There were houses, sunlight, and blood, but no people.

The distance was thudding heavily. The horizon was loose, perhaps, and was bumping on the earth. Ahead of us, almost lost in a clump of trees, were the red roofs of a farmhouse and its sheds. There were ragged gaps in the tiles. As we neared the farm there was a crash, as though a boiler plate had dropped from a great height to paving stones, and was at once still. Two columns of black smoke, which had not been there before, stood over the farm. Nevertheless, the road continued with indifference, though a tree had been lifted by the roots across it. There was a row of trees that had been reduced to bundles of white splinters, and near them we found the first men. Six of them lay in a row by a wall, and two others stood over them. The faces of the men on the ground were averted, and their eyes were closed. They did not want to look at us.

The ugly but intermittent sound of unseen bodies lumbering through the air was more frequent when we reached another group of buildings, scattered among trees at a road crossing. The trees were motionless in the sleeping afternoon. The walls of one of the barns, a structure so weathered that its rufous brickwork had the surface of crumbling grey stone, were riven, and the raw edges of the gaps were bright red. From somewhere came a noise which might have been made by an idle boy rattling a stick along a fence. An officer, to my surprise, then appeared at the door of a barn I had thought was empty. 'Come in,' he urged us. 'They spray that road with a machine-gun. Can't you hear it?' But for that distant rattling the silence was so deep that I imagined I could hear a frog I saw flopping across the road. A pair of swallows were circling about, and their familiar celerity and accuracy, as they pitched on their nest built under the eaves of a house on the point of collapse, had been regarded by me in confidence as tokens of the world I used to know.

Under the rafters of that partially dismantled barn was a man who laughed when he saw me. His amusement was caused, most likely, by my unexpected appearance, which he had to take as another absurd feature in a phantasy. He himself, an Oriental scholar, as a soldier in that place, was not easily believable. He laughed again because his quizzical temper, I suppose, thoroughly relished the waywardness of this coincidence.

'What brings you here? Have you gone potty, too?' he asked. He gossiped disjointedly about our circumstances. 'You may have noticed there is a war on up here, but who is making it, except ourselves, beats me. It's between us and the spooks, I think. You haven't noticed any so-called Germans hanging about, have you? I haven't seen one yet' – he flinched and grimaced at an explosion outside – 'but that sort of thing all day has to be accounted for.'

We left that barn. We set out together for his own place, which he said was near, though long before we reached it – mainly through a serpentining trench – my sense of direction went dizzy, and was sure only of up and down. The earth was crackling in the heat; that was rifle fire. The deep drain meandered aimlessly, with charlock and poppies vivid overhead against the sky. We climbed out to hurry across a road, and entered another drain, which burrowed among the ruins of buildings, and then we waited, on hands and knees, while the brickbats ahead of us were smashed a little more. When the dust and smoke were clearing we hurried along, and soon came out into a village.

It was abandoned. It was acrid with smoke and smouldering fires. There was a smell of damp earth and mortar. Some of the houses had fallen across the street. That village had come to its end, and the only proof that life had even known it was a child's doll sprawled in mimicry of wanton grief near the mummied carcase of a cow. We crossed the churchyard – one Gothic arch of the church was standing to frame daylight – and strode over grey rubble, splintered coffin boards, and a few resurrected sleepers in nightgowns who had risen from their graves indifferent as to where they slept. A spasmodic growling flew at us through the quiet and ended in a great clang by the Gothic arch. We descended hurriedly a long flight of stone steps to a cellar. My friend Upcott then sat on a packing box and laughed again, a little too long. 'This is my home,' he explained. 'I share it with a surgeon. I think he'll lend you a bed for the night.' Upcott pointed to a stretcher in a corner.

The cellar was spacious and gloomy, and our privacy was a corner of it, screened by some sacking from what Upcott named the Battalion Aid Post; that was the remainder of the cellar. We had the cellar to ourselves, then. Upcott was eager for news; yet even as I began to recount some to him our cellar began to shake in a series of spasms. A tin bowl on the floor trembled and whined. We waited, and soon the cellar sank deep into the quiet earth again.

'We're all right here,' Upcott speculated doubtfully, 'because if that stairway goes there is another way out. Perhaps I'd better show you where it is.'

We had a look round, and saw the other stairway, a pile of bandages, and wine bins containing nothing but a cat, which was pleased to meet us. Then there was no more to do except to return to the kitchen table. That was loaded with neat piles of documents, each pile under a shell-nose. Upcott took off his tunic, inspected a document, and filled his pipe.

'Now you've seen this place, perhaps you'd hardly believe the trouble I took to get from India to it,' he said. 'We heard that men were badly wanted, so I thought I ought to be quick, and I was. I got away from the mark in style, but the results surprised me. My patience had to mount a lot of monuments – it was patience which sat on a monument, wasn't it? – anyhow, I was kept waiting a devil of a time on each one I came to. After all, there was no hurry in this war. What a rummy old dear Authority always is! It tried to keep me from the delights of this beastly hole as long as possible. But one day I got to France. I was peeved, for I thought the war would be over before I could have some. Whelan!'

'Sir!'

'Whisky! Have you seen Major Weston today?'

'No, sir. He was killed last night, sir.'

Upcott rose and stared at me. Then he sat down again. 'Bring the drinks, Whelan,' he said.

He sat, turning his pipe round and round, as though examining it for a defect, whilst he frowned. Then he spoke to himself. 'I suppose it's right.' He muttered across to me in doubt. 'I tell you I spoke to him last night. I spoke to him.' He appeared to invite my confirmation that a little conversation with another man might at times fail to render him invulnerable.

The servant returned, methodical as at a London counter, and then vanished as though he had passed through a wall.

'They end like that,' said Upcott. 'There they are, and then they're not; but the war goes on . . . for how long, do you think? . . . I say, I wish I had no sense, then I might enjoy it.'

Upcott remained pensive for so long that his pipe went out. Then he walked to the other end of the cellar and back. He lit his pipe again, and sat down. 'I came here in such an infernal hurry, in case I missed it. You might as well worry over not being late for your funeral.

'They shunted me about France for weeks in trains and lorries – I couldn't find my lot – I thought the battalion I'd been sent to didn't exist. Everybody knew at once where it was, but it was never there, though sometimes it had been. At last I did find it, and reported myself. The adjutant said, "But where's your sword? You can't parade without a sword." So I went to a farm, and sent to London for a sword, and slept in an outhouse under the chickens while waiting for it. Then the sword came, and I reported myself again. "You've got a sword," said the adjutant. "You cannot parade with a sword. The order is to return all swords."

'That's what it's like,' Upcott assured me. 'Its all like that. I tell you there's only one thing to do here – shut off your intelligence.

Kill your memories. Forget everything you ever learned, forget your friends, write them off. They don't exist. Hope the next thing to happen won't be as silly as everything that has happened before. If you try to be reasonable here you get into a frightful mess. One day one of the headquarters – I dunno which, brigade, division, corps, army, or else the holy of holies – wanted to know why we were using so much chloride of lime. I suppose they thought we were eating it. Perhaps headquarters don't have to use chloride of lime. Anyhow, I wrote across the requisition, "latrines and drinking water".

'Lord, we wanted a disinfectant then, my son. My truthful reply tore it. Believe me, there was a stink. The colonel got worried. He said I'd better send an officer to the latrines just to satisfy the holy of holies with a nice report. That officer was gone too long about it. I got nervous, and had to go after him. There had been some nasty shelling, you know. His runner was lying wounded by the latrines, and there was the subaltern . . . well, we wanted more chloride of lime, then.'

Upcott's narrative was interrupted here. I heard a scuffling on the stairs, and a whispering.

'You take 'is legs.'

'I gottim.'

A little group of Tommies then moved across the cellar, and laid one of their number on a bench. The others arranged themselves along the same form in various attitudes of lassitude and indifference. They were muddy, gaunt and unshaven. Several of them attempted cigarettes, yet with a sluggishness which allowed a match to burn out before it was used.

Upcott, after a steady glance at that array of cripples now composed, lax and still, called out that the medical officer was expected back at once. One of them lifted reproachful eyes to us, but none of them spoke nor moved. Other footsteps sounded on the stairs, hard and deliberate, and the M.O. and two men entered. Upcott adjusted the canvas screen, watched round the edge of it for a moment, called out that if help were wanted we were there, and then came to sit beside me on his box.

'That goes on all day, off and on. When they're really busy it's no place for me – I can't stand being looked at like that. I don't care for the colour of that fellow on his back, do you? His feet are too loose. Sometimes a man's feet tell you more than his face.'

We heard groans, and Upcott paused. We sat, looking at the floor.

'No.' (It was the decisive voice of the M.O.) 'No. Leave that man. You men all right now? Feel you can do it? Then make your way out while it's quiet. Lucky beggars. Hop it. Off you go.'

The shuffling began anew, and when it had ceased we heard the M.O. coldly instructing his assistants where they were to put the soldier who had to stay. The doctor came over for a gossip before venturing forth; and then again we had the gloom to ourselves.

'Can you make anything of it?' asked Upcott, with an inconsequence which was not quite innocent.

'It is a little queer.'

'Queer? You may well say it. Queer, eh? There's no sense in it. We're all daft. We're all up in the air. Those fellows who have just gone out to hobble through shell-bursts trusting to luck – what do they make of it? What patient lads they are. They never say a word. I shouldn't have thought men could be so patient, but between you and me they're damned fools, and it's a good thing for us they are. We'd be in a fix if they had any sense. It's all our doing, you know, all this. We're the governing classes, aren't we? Sorry; I don't know whether you belong but I do. I'm one of the rulers of India, in case you haven't noticed it. I tell you I wonder those fellows don't round on us, for the bungling duffers we are. That would stop it. They ought to right about face all along the front, and march on London, Paris and Berlin. That would be fixing it where it belonged; but they'll never do it, never. No, they never say a word. They'll never do anything except kill each other. When I see what good-natured lads they are, and the way they stick the worst of this job, I feel I could hug them first and kick them afterwards. They're like the horses. Do what they're told. Never say anything. But some of the horses sweat through funk. Once a horse has had a dose of it, he begins to sweat whenever he hears a bump. Trembles and sweats.

But he goes into it when ordered, all of a lather, and so do we – all of a lather. Heroic fatheads!'

'When I was getting here today,' I told Upcott, 'I got the notion that the whole thing was an illusion. The country is hardly real. I began to wonder whether it was there, or whether I was there. Perhaps these men . . .'

'I know. That's what does it. Most of us feel that way. We reckon we're in a dream, and can't wake up because we are awake. But you'd better not be fooled by it. It is real – as real as this cellar. At first you think it's rather a silly joke. You laugh at it. That's why some of the best of the young 'uns die too soon. They hardly believe it. They go about showing it no respect. But there it is all right, and it gets them. It may look like moonshine, but we're caught in it all right, and so you'll jolly well find. Look, here comes its Hermes.'

A despatch rider entered, saluted, handed out of the blue his token, and went. Upcott read the message, sighed, and placed it on one of the neat piles.

'You get the notion,' he said, 'that anyhow you are lost in it. Nobody knows where you are, and nobody could ever find you. Wrong again! The gods have got us taped. They know where we are, and all about us, and if they order you to put your head in a bag you've got to do it. You can die here for two reasons – for being an idiot, and for refusing to be an idiot.

'The things that happen here – there never is any sense in them. They just happen. One day, when we had got back to rest billets – our rest was shelled to hell most of the time – the colonel came to me. "Look here," he said. "Here's something from the general. It says a French colonel is going to visit us, though it doesn't say what he wants – just to see our little lot, I suppose – and we've got to treat him mighty fine. Look here, we've got no food fit to eat, and he'll be here tonight. Just scout for something tasty, will you? Luckily we can make him drunk, if he's that sort of chap. And I say, I wish you'd let him have your bed. His adjutant will be with him, and he can have mine, as yours is the best."

'I tell you, we cursed those Frenchmen for nuisances, but we made ready for them, and our mess cook turned out a really presentable table. Then we waited for them, wondering what was the correct form for such an occasion, because we'd seen nothing of the French in the war, so far. Immensely impressed, of course, by their reputation, and all that. They were soldiers, and most of us were only civilians trying to be. Our adjutant was the most likely specimen we had. Even our colonel didn't look like a colonel – a stout man, though. We were a bit nervous about this visit.

'Presently he rolled up, this French johnny – a big fellow, with a tummy on him, in a blue uniform and brown bulging gaiters. Behind him was a slender young officer, very stiff and correct. The French colonel had one of those hunting horns round his shoulder – you know the sort of thing – you see it in comic prints of French sportsmen – a curly trumpet – they go out after partridge with it, don't they? Well, he didn't take that trumpet off him. Only his cap. His bald head was pale, but his big round face was rosy and very happy, with lots of chin, and a long grizzled moustache which would have been straight and fierce if he hadn't laughed so much. He did laugh. He stamped with one foot, and patted his tummy with both hands, and laughed very free and hearty, and then hummed and pulled out his moustache. A cheery card. But his young officer was prim. He didn't laugh at anything. Never said a word. Smiled faintly and loftily when spoken to. "Yes," he said. Only that. He was supercilious. Thought we were rather a bore, I believe.

'Not a word did they give us about the object of their visit – just rich laughter from the colonel over nothing in particular. We began dinner. The French colonel wore his hunting horn. Of course, we pretended not to see the thing – sort of behaved as though we were used to that at dinner – custom of the country, you know. The young officer, he hardly looked up, or if he did it was only to screw his eyes at the wall over the head of the man opposite. That chap ate our food as if he had to do it. Duty was duty, and we were only British, and didn't know any better.

'But his colonel was all right. He was different. He enjoyed himself – we happened to have a Burgundy of a good year – and our fellows played up to him for the good of the regiment. After one burst of merriment, which was so hearty that we all joined in, that big Frenchman rose, put one foot on his chair, and tootled his hunting horn.

'Not likely we took any notice of it. Not likely. Too well-trained. Pretended we heard nothing. The young Frenchman, he took no notice of it. I supposed this tootling might be the custom of the regiment of our visitors, an ancient right won in battle. It was the proper thing for the colonel of that regiment to do – blow his blessed horn at intervals during dinner. He had to maintain a link with the glorious past.

'He was a lusty chap, our important guest. Full of beans and funny stories. At the end of a cheery one, when he'd got us all going, he'd rise from his chair, and solemnly let go a tantara. Our servants were good lads – they did seem a bit surprised, but they never laughed. As for our own old man, he was so polite that he might have been as deaf to that hunting horn as the young French officer.

'After dinner the fun got very lively. I must say our youngsters thoroughly enjoyed this Gascon, who certainly was enjoying himself. He approved our whisky. Then he got into a sentimental mood; he mentioned his wife. Ah! He would show why France would fight, gentlemen, till not a German was this side of the Rhine; that or death. He became serious. Gentlemen, you shall observe this. He put a hand inside his tunic, and tugged at what I thought was a pack of cards. But the pack was tight, and he tugged too hard. The cards shot across the table. Well, I was a bit shocked. I'll admit it. Photographs of women! And some of them! You never saw such a collection of bosoms and behinds. Do you think that fine old fellow was embarrassed? Not a scrap. It was the sort of thing that might happen to any good man, if he were clumsy with his pocket-book. He began to sort them, coolly and indifferently, sort of shuffling the pack, perhaps looking for the queen of hearts – I dunno.

'Then for the first time that evening the severe young Frenchman condescended to take an interest in what was going on. He rose, and leaned over the table, intently inspecting the pictorial assortment of ladies. His curiosity was genuine. Suddenly he pointed sharply at a photograph. He spoke at last. "That is my wife," he said to his colonel.

'He punched his colonel in the eye. The big fellow collided with a chair behind him, and over it went, and so did he, with a frightful banging of brassware on the stone floor. Our own colonel was horrified. We were all alarmed. We stared at one another. What happened when a French officer punched his colonel in the eye? What ought we to do when they were our guests? There's nothing in the King's Regulations about that, is there?

'One of our fellows was assisting the jolly Frenchman to his feet, but he sprang up, shook with laughter as he pulled his tunic straight, and went out into the yard. Outside, we heard him play a bold fanfare on his horn – a salute to all stags, I suppose. He was soon back.

'As he entered he was met by his junior. They embraced each other, and kissed. I looked away at our colonel. I didn't know where to look. Our old man stood as if he were frightened. He stood at the fireplace, fumbling badly at his moustache. Fact is, the lot of us supported the old country pretty well, I think. Nobody acted as though he'd seen anything out of the way – sort of thing which might happen in any well-regulated mess in war-time, don't you know.

'I lost count of the time that night, but I remember helping the big fellow to bed. When the pair of them had gone none of us said a word about the evening's performance. Oh, one of the young 'uns did speak. He said to the colonel, "Do you think he plays that trumpet in bed, sir?" But our colonel said nothing. We put out the lights.

'Next morning at breakfast we were very moody. The Frenchmen were a long time coming down, but nobody said so. I rather think we were in doubt. What had happened the night before? After a bit our colonel called across to me. "Look here, Upcott, I'm right, am I not? There were two Frenchmen with us last night?"

' "Yes, sir, I think so. I had that impression myself, but as nobody else owned up to it I thought I'd better keep quiet."

' "Right," said the colonel. "That settles it. If they were here then, they're here now. Come along, Upcott, come and greet them."

'We went to our colonel's room first, where we'd put the adjutant. He wasn't there, though the bed had been slept in. Then we toddled along to my room. No French colonel, either. Nothing there, except a hunting horn, hung round a knob of my bed. "Well, I'm damned," said our old man.

'And it's a funny thing, but none of our orderlies saw those fellows go. And we never heard any more about it. Not a word. What do you make of it?'

I did not attempt to make anything of it. As an episode of the war it was as meet and proper as an Oriental scholar making British reports on the local use of chloride of lime in the cellar of a French farm. While Upcott and I sat smiling at each other, filling our pipes, the tin bowl on the floor woke up; it began to complain again. It trembled and whined. The cellar became convulsive. The cat galloped up to us, and stood staring, in alert suspicion, at the bare wall behind us. Somebody fell headlong down the stairs.

H. M. TOMLINSON was born in 1873 in the East End of London and grew up in Dockland, starting work at the age of twelve as a clerk in a shipping company. He became a full-time writer at the age of thirty-one on the *Morning Leader*, and a war correspondent on the Western Front in 1914. He won the *Femina-Vie Heureuse* prize for 1927 with his novel *Gallions Reach*. His *All Our Yesterdays* maintained his reputation, but most of his works are sea stories.

THE BATTLE OF THE MIST

Bartimeus

Thorogood, Lieutenant of the Afternoon Watch, climbed the ladder to the upper bridge as the bell struck the half-hour after noon. A blue worsted muffler, gift and handiwork of an aunt on the outbreak of war, enfolded his neck. He wore a pair of glasses in a case slung over one shoulder and black leather gauntlet gloves.

The Officer of the Forenoon Watch, known among his messmates as Tweedledee, was focussing the range-finder on the ship ahead of them in the line; he looked round as the newcomer appeared, and greeted him with a grin.

'Hullo, James,' he said. 'Your afternoon watch? Well, here you are.' He made a comprehensive gesture embracing the vast Fleet that was spread out over the waters as far as the eye could reach.

'Divisions in line ahead, columns disposed abeam, course S.E. Speed, fifteen knots. Glass low and steady. The Cruisers are ahead

The battle cruiser Queen Mary *sinks beneath a plume of smoke during the Battle of Jutland, 31 May 1916.*

there, beyond the Destroyers,' he nodded ahead. 'But you can't see them because of the mist. The Battle-cruisers are somewhere beyond them again, with their Light Cruisers and Destroyers – about thirty miles to the southward. The hands are at dinner and all is peace. She's keeping station quite well now.' The speaker moved to the range-finder again and peered into it at the next ahead. 'Right to a yard, James.'

Thorogood nodded. 'Thank you : I hope I'll succeed in keeping her there. Any news?'

'News?' The other laughed. 'What about?'

'Well,' replied Thorogood, 'the perishing Hun, let's say.'

The Navigator, thoughtfully biting the end of a pencil, came out of the chart-house with a note-book in his hand, in which he had been working out the noon reckoning.

'Pilot,' said the departing Officer of the Forenoon Watch, 'James is thirsting for news of the enemy.'

'Optimist!' replied the Navigator composedly. 'News, indeed! This isn't Wolff's Agency, my lad. This is a Cook's tour of the North Sea.' He sniffed the damp, salt breeze. 'Bracing air, change of scenery : no undue excitement – sort of rest cure, in fact. And you come along exhibiting a morbid craving for excitement.'

'I know,' said Thorogood meekly. 'It's the effect of going to the cinematograph. All the magistrates are talking about it. They say Charlie Chaplin's got something to do with it. I suppose, though, there's no objection to my asking what the disposition of our Light Cruisers happens to be, is there? It's prompted more by a healthy desire to improve my knowledge before I take over the afternoon watch than anything else.'

'They're out on the starboard quarter,' replied the late Officer of the Watch. 'You can't see them because of this cursed mist, but they're there.'

'Strikes me this afternoon watch is going to be more of a faith cure than a rest cure as the Pilot suggests,' grumbled Thorogood. 'Battle-cruisers somewhere ahead, Cruisers invisible in the mist, Light Cruisers – '

The report of a gun, followed almost instantly by a loud explosion, came from far away on the port bow. A Destroyer that had altered course was resuming her position in the Destroyer line on the outskirts of the Fleet. A distant column of smoke and spray was slowly dissolving into the North Sea haze.

At the report of the gun the three men raised their glasses to stare in the direction of the sound. 'Only one of the Huns' floating mines,' said the Navigator. 'She exploded it with her three-pounder. Pretty shot.'

'Well,' said Tweedledee, 'I can't stay here all day. Anything else you want to know, James? What's for lunch, I'm devilish hungry.'

'Boiled beef and carrots,' replied Thorogood. '*Mit* apple tart and cream: the Messman can't be well. Pills says it's squandomania. No, I don't think I want to know any more. I suppose the log's written up?'

'It is. Now for the boiled beef, and this afternoon Little Brighteyes is going to get his head down and have a nice sleep.'

The speaker prepared to depart.

'Hold on,' said the Navigator. 'I'm coming with you. I've just got to give the noon position to the Owner on the way.'

They descended the ladder together, and left Thorogood alone on the platform.

The Battle-fleet was steaming in parallel lines about a mile apart, each Squadron in the wake of its Flagship. The Destroyers, strung out on either flank of the Battle-fleet, were rolling steadily in the long, smooth swell, leaving a smear of smoke in their trail. Far away in the mist astern flickered a very bright light: the invisible Light Cruisers must be there, reflected Thorogood, and presently from the Fleet Flagship came a succession of answering blinks. The light stopped flickering out of the mist.

The speed at which the Fleet was travelling sent the wind thrumming through the halliards and funnel stays and past Thorogood's ears with a little whistling noise; otherwise few sounds reached him at the altitude at which he stood. On the signal-platform below, a number of signalmen were grouped round the flag-lockers with the halliards in their hands in instant readiness to hoist a signal. The Signal Boatswain had steadied his glass against a semaphore, and was studying something on the misty outskirts of the Fleet. The Quartermaster at the wheel was watching the compass card with a silent intensity that made his face look as if it had been carved in bronze. The telegraph-men maintained a conversation that was pitched in a low, deep note inaudible two yards away. It concerned the photograph of a mutual lady acquaintance, and has no place in this narrative.

Thorogood moved to the rail and looked down at the familiar forecastle and teeming upper-deck, thirty feet below. Seen thus from above, the grey, sloping shields of the turrets, each with its great twin guns, looked like gigantic mythical tortoises with two heads and disproportionately long necks. It was the dinner hour, and men were moving about, walking up and down, or sitting about in little groups smoking. Some were playing cards in places sheltered from the wind and spray; near the blacksmith's forge a man was stooping patiently over a small black object: Thorogood raised his glasses for a moment and recognized the ship's cat, reluctantly undergoing instruction in jumping through the man's hands.

The cooks of the Messes were wending their way in procession to the chutes at the ship's sides, carrying mess-kettles containing scraps and slops from the mess-deck dinner. For an instant the Officer of the Watch, looking down from that altitude and cut off from all sounds but that of the wind, experienced a feeling of unfamiliar detachment from the pulsating mass of metal beneath his feet. He had a vision of the electric-lit interior of the great ship, deck beneath deck, with men everywhere. Men rolled up in coats and oilskins, snatching half-an-hour's sleep along the crowded gun-batteries, men writing letters to sweethearts and wives, men laughing and quarrelling, or singing low-toned, melancholy ditties as they mended worn garments: hundreds and hundreds of reasoning human entities were crowded in those steel-walled spaces, each with his boundless hopes and affections, his separate fears and vices and conceptions of the Deity, and his small, incommunicable distresses. . . .

Beneath all that again, far below the surface of the grey North Sea, were men, moving about purring turbines and dynamos and webs of stupendous machinery, silently oiling, testing and adjusting a thousand moving joints of metal. There were adjoining caverns lit by the glare of furnaces that shone red on the glistening faces of men, silent vaults and passages where the projectiles were ranged in sinister array, and chilly spaces in which the electric light was reflected from the burnished and oiled torpedoes that hung in readiness above the submerged tubes.

Thorogood raised his eyes and stared out across the vast array of the Battle-fleet. Obedient to the message flashed from the Flagship a few minutes earlier, the Light Cruisers that had been invisible on the quarter now emerged from behind the curtain of the mist and were rapidly moving up to a new position. Presently the same mysterious, soundless voice spoke again :

YOU ARE MAKING TOO MUCH SMOKE

blinked the glittering searchlight, and anon in the stokeholds of the end ship of the lee line there was the stokehold equivalent for weeping and wailing and the gnashing of teeth. . . .

For a couple of hours the Fleet surged onwards in silence and unchanged formation. The swift Light Cruisers had overtaken the advancing Battle-fleet, and vanished like wraiths into the haze ahead.

The Captain and the Navigator had joined Thorogood on the bridge, and were poring over the chart and talking in low voices. The Midshipman of the Watch stood with eyes glued to the range-finder, turning his head at intervals to report the distance of the next ahead to the Officer of the Watch.

A messenger from the Coding Officer tumbled pell-mell up the ladder and handed a piece of folded paper to the Captain, saluted, turned on his heel and descended the ladder again. The Captain unfolded the signal and read with knitted brows. Then he turned quickly to the chart again.

For a moment he was busy with dividers and parallel-rulers; when he raised his head his eyes were alight with a curiously restrained excitement.

'Rather interesting,' he said, and passed the paper to the Navigator who read it in turn and grinned like a schoolboy.

'They have probably caught a raiding party in the mist, sir,' he said, and bent over the chart.

Thorogood picked up the message and pursed his lips up in a short, soundless whistle.

'It's too much to hope that their main fleet's out,' he said.

'Their main fleet's sure to be in support somewhere,' replied the Captain. 'It's a question whether they realize we're all down on top of 'em, though, and nip for home before we catch them.'

A second messenger flung himself, panting, up the ladder, and handed in a second message.

'Intercepted wireless to Flag, sir.'

The Captain read it and took a breath that was like a sigh of relief. 'At last!' he said.

The Navigator turned from the chart.

'*Der Tag*, sir?' he asked interrogatively with a smile.

The Captain nodded ahead at the haze curtaining all the horizon. 'If we catch 'em,' he replied.

The signal platform was awhirl with bunting; the voice of the Chief Yeoman repeating hoists rose above the stamp of feet and the flapping of flags in the wind.

Thorogood turned to the Navigator. 'Will you take on now?' he asked in a low voice. 'If the balloon's really going up this time I'd better get along to my battery.'

As he descended the ladder the upper-deck was ringing with bugle-calls, and the turrets' crews were already swarming round their guns. From the hatchways leading to the lower-deck came a great roar of cheering. Men poured up on their way to their action stations in a laughing, rejoicing throng. Mouldy Jakes, with the ever-faithful Midshipman of his turret at his side, was hurrying to his beloved guns, and greeted Thorogood as he passed with a sidelong jerk of the head and the first whole-souled smile of enjoyment a mess-mate had ever surprised on his face. Further aft the Captain of Marines was standing on the roof of his slowly revolving turret:

'Buck up, James,' he shouted merrily. ' "Johnnie, get your gun, there's a cat in the garden"—we're going to see Life in a minute, my lad!'

He was right, but they were also destined to see Death, holding red carnival.

Thorogood waved his arm and shouted an inarticulate reply as he ran aft to the hatchway leading to the cabin flat. Officers were rushing past on their way to their posts, exchanging chaff and conjecture as they went. Thorogood descended to the cabin flat, jerked back the curtain of his cabin, and hurriedly entered the familiar apartment. Opening a drawer he snatched up a gas-mask and a packet containing first-aid appliances which he thrust into the pocket of his swimming waistcoat, together with a flask and a small tin of compressed meat lozenges. Once before, earlier in the war, he had fought for life clinging to a floating spar. Then succour had come in a comparatively short time, but the experience had not been without its lesson.

He made for the door again and then paused on the threshold hesitatingly. 'Might as well,' he said, and turning back picked up a small photograph in a folding morocco frame and thrust it half-shamefacedly into an inside pocket.

As he emerged into the flat again he met Gerrard, the Assistant Paymaster, struggling into a thick coat outside the door of his cabin.

'Hullo!' laughed the A.P. 'Having a last look at the old home, James?'

Thorogood patted his pockets. 'Just taking in provisions in case I have to spend the week-end on a raft. What's your action station?'

'Fore-top,' was the reply. 'Taking notes of the action. Now, have I got everything? Thermos flask – watch – note-book – glasses – right! *En avant, mon brave!*'

Thorogood reached the 6-inch battery breathless, and found the guns' crews busy tricing up their mess-tables overhead. The Gunner was passing along the crowded deck ahead of him. He stopped opposite the after gun:

'They're out, lads!' he said grimly. 'Give 'em hell, this time. Clear away and close up round your guns – smartly then, my hearties!'

From the other side of the deck came the voice of Tweedledee giving orders to his battery, raised above the clatter of the ammunition hoists, the thud of projectiles as they were placed in the rear of each gun, the snap and clang of the breech as the guns were loaded. . . .

Fire and wreckage parties stood in little groups along the main-deck, and first-aid parties were gathered at the hatchways; two Midshipmen, pale and bright-eyed with excitement, talked in low voices by the foremost gun: gradually a tense hush closed down upon the main deck; the crews stood silent round their guns, waiting in their steel-walled casemates for the signal that would galvanize them into death-dealing activity against the invisible foe.

Ultimate victory no man doubted: death might sweep, swift and shattering, along these electric-lit enclosed spaces where they stood waiting; the great ship was being driven headlong by unseen forces towards an unseen foe. But of that foe, none of the hundreds of men between decks save the straining gunlayers with their eyes at the sighting-telescopes would ever catch a single glimpse.

The silence was riven by a roaring concussion that seemed to shake the framework of the ship. The great turret guns on the upper deck had opened fire with a salvo, and, as if released by the explosion, a burst of frantic cheering leaped from every throat and echoed and reverberated along the decks. Somewhere in the outside world of mist and sea, under the grey Northern sky, the Battle-fleet action had begun.

The fore-top was a semi-circular eyrie, roofed and walled with steel, that projected from the fore topmast some distance above the giant tripod. It was reached by iron rungs let into the mast, and here Gerrard, with the din of bugles and the cheering still ringing in his ears, joined the assembled officers and men whose station it was in action.

From that dizzy elevation it was possible to take in the disposition of the vast Fleet at a single glance. It was like looking down on model ships spread out over a grey carpet preparatory to a children's game. A white flicker of foam at each blunt ram and the wind singing past the hooded top alone gave any indication of the speed at which the ships were advancing. It was an immense monochrome of grey. Grey ships with the White Ensign flying free on each: grey sea flecked here and there by the diverging bow-waves breaking as they met: a grey sky along which the smoke trailed sullenly and gathered in a dense, low-lying cloud that mingled with the haze astern.

The Lieutenant in the top drew Gerrard to his side. 'Put your head down here,' he said, 'out of the wind . . . can you hear?' There was a queer ring of exultation in his voice. 'Guns!'

Gerrard bent down and strained all his faculties to listen. For a moment he heard nothing but the hum of the wind and the vibration of the engines transmitted by the mast. Then, faint and intermittent, like the far-off grumble of a gathering thunderstorm, his ears caught a sound that sent all his pulses hammering.

'Thank God I've lived to hear that noise!' muttered the Lieutenant. He straightened up, staring ahead through his glasses in the direction of the invisible fight.

For a while no one spoke. The tense minutes dragged by as the sounds of firing grew momentarily more distinct. The uncertain outline of the near horizon was punctuated by vivid flashes of flame from the guns of the approaching enemy. They were still hidden by the mist and apparently unconscious of the Battle-fleet bearing down upon them like some vast, implacable instrument of doom. The target of their guns suddenly became visible as the Battle-cruisers appeared on the starboard bow, moving rapidly across the limit of vision like a line of grey phantoms spitting fire and destruction as they went. Misty columns of foam that leaped up from the water all about them showed that they were under heavy fire.

The Battle-fleet were deploying into Line of Battle, Squadron forming up astern of Squadron in a single line of mailed monsters extending far into the haze that was momentarily closing in upon them. The curtain ahead was again pierced by a retreating force of Cruisers beaten back on the protection of the Battle-fleet and ringed by leaping waterspouts as the enemy's salvos pursued them.

As yet the enemy were invisible, but when the last ship swung into deployment the mist cleared for a moment and disclosed them amid a cloud of smoke and the furious flashes of guns. The moment had come, and all along the extended British battle-line the turret guns opened fire with a roar of angry sound that seemed to split the grey vault of heaven. As if to mock them in that supreme instant the mist swirled across again and hid the German Fleet wheeling round in panic flight.

The gases belched from the muzzles of the guns, together with the smoke of hundreds of funnels caught and held by the encircling mist, reeled to and fro across the spouting water and mingled with the grey clouds from bursting shell. Through it all the two Fleets, the pursuing and the pursued, grappled in blindfold headlong fury.

Thorogood's battery was on the disengaged side of the ship during the earlier phases of the action. Across the deck they heard the guns of Tweedledee's battery open fire with a roar, and then the cheering of the crews, mingled with the cordite fumes, was drowned by an ear-splitting detonation in the confined spaces of the mess deck, followed by a blinding flash of light.

Tweedledee was flung from where he was standing to pitch brokenly at the foot of the hatchway, like a rag doll flung down by a child in a passion. He lay outstretched, face downwards, with his head resting on his forearm as if asleep. Most of the lights had been extinguished by the explosion, but a pile of cartridges in the rear of one of the guns had caught fire and burned fiercely, illuminating everything was a yellow glare.

Lettigne, Midshipman of the battery, was untouched; deafened and deathly sick he took command of the remaining guns. He, who ten seconds before had never even seen death, was slithering about dimly-lit decks, slippery with what he dared not look at, encourageing and steadying the crews, and helping to extinguish the burning cordite. In darkened corners, where they had been thrown by the explosion, men were groaning and dying. . . .

That shell had been one of several that had struck the ship simultaneously. Mouldy Jakes opened his eyes to see a streak of light showing through a jagged rip in a bulkhead. The light was red and hurt his eyes: he passed his hand across his face, and it was wet with a warm stickiness. His vision cleared, however, and for a few moments he studied the drops of water that were dripping from the gash in the plating. 'Crying!' he said stupidly. The shells that pitched short had deluged the fore-part of the ship with water, and it was still dripping into the interior of the turret. Mouldy Jakes raised his head, and a yard or two away saw Morton. The breech of one of the guns was open, and Morton was lying limply over the huge breech-block. The machinery was smashed and twisted, and mixed up with it were dead men and bits of men. . . .

A little while later the Fleet Surgeon, splashed with red to the elbows, glanced up from his work in the fore-distributing station and saw a strange figure descending the hatchway. It was Mouldy Jakes: his scalp was torn so that a red triangular patch hung rakishly over one eye. Flung over his shoulder was the limp form of an unconscious Midshipman. For a moment he stood swaying, steadying himself with outstretched hand against the rail of the ladder.

'Thought I'd better bring him along,' he gasped. 'Turret's knocked to hell. . . . He's still alive, but he's broken all to little bits inside . . . I can feel him . . . Morton, snottie of my turret . . .'

Sickberth Stewards relieved him of his burden, and Mouldy Jakes sat down on the bottom rung of the ladder and began to whimper like a distraught child. 'It's my hand . . .' he said plaintively, and extended a trembling, shattered palm. 'I've only just noticed it.'

With his eye glued to the periscope of his turret the India-rubber Man was fidgeting and swearing softly under his breath at the exasperating treachery of the fog. The great guns under his control roared at intervals, but before the effect of the shell-burst could be observed the enemy would be swallowed from sight. Once, at the commencement of the action, he thought of Betty; he thought of her tenderly and reverently, and then put her out of his mind. . . .

Lanes of unexpected visibility opened while an eyelid winked, and disclosed a score of desperate fights passing and reappearing like scenes upon a screen. A German Battleship, near and quite distinct, was in sight for a moment, listing slowly over with her guns pointing upwards like the fingers of a distraught hand, and as she sank the mist closed down again as it were a merciful curtain drawn to hide a horror. An enemy Cruiser dropped down the engaged side of the line like an exhausted participator in a Bacchanal of Furies. Her sides were riven and gaping, with a red glare showing through the rents. Her decks were a ruined shambles of blackened, twisted metal, but she still spat defiance from a solitary gun, and sank firing as the fight swept past.

Hither and thither rolled the fog, blotting out the enemy at one moment, at another disclosing swift and awful cataclysms. A British Cruiser, dodging and zigzagging through a tempest of shells, blew up. She changed on the instant into a column of black smoke and wreckage that leaped up into the outraged sky; it trembled there like a dark monument to the futile hate of man for his brother man and slowly dissolved into the mist. A German Destroyer attack crumpled up in the blast of the 6-inch batteries of the British Fleet, and the British Destroyers dashed to meet their crippled onslaught as vultures might swoop on blinded wolves. They fought at point-blank range, asking no quarter, expecting none; they fought over decks ravaged by shrapnel and piled with dead. The sea was thick with floating corpses and shattered wreckage, and darkened with patches of oil that marked the grave of a rammed Submarine or sunken Destroyer. Maimed and bleeding men dragged themselves on to rafts and cheered their comrades as they left them to their death.

Through that witches' cauldron of fog and shell-smoke the British Battle-fleet groped for its elusive foe. One minute of perfect visibility, one little minute of clear range beyond the fog-masked sights, was all they asked to deal the death-blow that would end the fight – men prayed God for it and died with the prayer in their teeth.

But the minute never came. The firing died away down the line; the dumb guns moved blindly towards the shifting sounds of strife like monsters mouthing for the prey that was denied them, but the fog held and the merciful dusk closed down and covered the flight of the stricken German Fleet for the shelter of its protecting mine-fields.

It was not until night fell that the British Destroyers began their savage work in earnest. Flotilla after flotilla was detached from the

Fleet and swallowed by the short summer night, moving swiftly and relentlessly to their appointed tasks like black panthers on the trail.

Cut off from their base by the British Fleet the scattered German squadrons dodged and doubled through the darkness, striving to elude the cordon drawn across their path. They can be pictured as towering black shadows rushing headlong through the night, with the wounded groaning between their wreckage-strewn decks: and on each bridge, high above them in the windy darkness, men talked in guttural monosyllables, peering through high-power glasses for the menace that stalked them. . . . On the trigger of every gun there would be a twitching finger, and all the while the blackness round them would be pierced and rent by distant spurts of flame. . . .

The wind and sea had risen, and over an area of several hundred square miles of stormy sea swept the Terror by Night. Bursting starshell and questioning searchlight fought with the darkness, betraying to the guns the sinister black hulls driving through clouds of silver spray, the loaded tubes and streaming decks, the oilskin-clad figures on each bridge forcing the attack home against the devastating blast of the shrapnel. Death was abroad, berserk and blindfold. A fleeing German Cruiser fell among a flotilla of Destroyers and altered her helm, with every gun and searchlight blazing, to ram the leading boat. The Destroyer had time to alter course sufficiently to bring the two ships bow to bow before the impact came. Then there was a grinding crash: forecastle, bridge and foremost gun a pile of wreckage and struggling figures. The blast of the German guns swept the funnels, boats, cowls and men away as a gale blows dead leaves before it. Then the Cruiser swung clear and vanished into the darkness, pursued by the remainder of the Flotilla, and leaving the Destroyer reeling among the waves like a man that has been struck in the face with a knuckle-duster by a runaway thief. In the direction where the Cruiser had disappeared five minutes later a column of flame leaped skyward, and the Flotilla, vengeance accomplished, swung off through the darkness in search of a fresh quarry.

All night long the disabled Destroyer rolled helplessly in the trough of the sea. The dawn came slowly across the sky, as if apprehensive of what it might behold on the face of the troubled waters; in the growing light the survivors of the Destroyer's crew saw a crippled German Cruiser trailing south at slow speed. Only one gun remained in action on board the Destroyer, and round that gathered the bandaged remnant of what had once been a ship's company. They shook hands grimly among themselves and spat and girded their loins for their last fight.

The German Cruiser turned slowly over and sank while they trained the gun. . . .

A dismasted Destroyer, with riddled funnels and a foot of water swilling across the floor plates in the engine-room, bore down upon them about noon and took her crippled sister in tow. They passed slowly away to the westward, leaving the circle of grey, tumbling sea to the floating wreckage of a hundred fights and the thin keening of the gulls.

The afternoon wore on : five drenched, haggard men were laboriously propelling a life-saving raft by means of paddles in the direction of the English coast that lay some hundred odd miles to the west. The waves washed over their numbed bodies, and imparted an almost lifelike air of animation to the corpse of a companion that lay between them, staring at the sullen sky.

Suddenly one of the paddlers stopped and pointed ahead. A boat manned by four men appeared on the crest of a wave and slid down a grey-back towards them. The oarsmen were rowing with slow strokes, and eventually the two craft passed each other within hailing distance. The men on the raft stared hard.

' 'Uns !' said one. 'Bloody 'Uns. . . . Strictly speakin', we did ought to fight 'em. . . . Best look t'other way, lads !'

His companions followed his example and continued their futile mechanical paddling with averted heads.

The bow-oar of the German boat, who had a blood-stained bandage round his head, also stared.

'*Engländer!*' he said. '*Verdammte Schweine!*' and added, '*Fünf!* . . .' whereupon he and his companions also averted their heads, because they were four.

They passed each other thus. The waves that washed over the raft rolled the dead man's head to and fro, as if he found the situation rather preposterous.

From: *The Long Trick.*

'*BARTIMEUS*' (Lewis Anselm da Costa Ricci) served in the Royal Navy throughout the 1914–18 War. He is the author of some twenty books, mainly sea or war stories.

THE MINE

'Sapper'

'Last night we exploded a mine under a redoubt in the enemy's trenches, and successfully occupied the crater. A considerable number of Germans were killed.' Thus the official communiqué.

And yet the great powers that be have no idea that this small local success was entirely due to David Jones – sometime miner in a coal-field in South Wales. In fact, the betting is about a fiver to an acid drop that they have no idea that he exists. Bar the police in his local village, who disliked him intensely, and his N.C.O.s out here, who disliked him still more, very few people do know that he exists. Undersized, in every way an undesirable acquaintance, a silent and morose man, it is neverthtless an undoubted fact that had it not been for David Jones, the aforementioned crater would not have been occupied, and the considerable number of

Battle of Albert: soldiers are laying a charge, and the officer on the left has a geophone around his neck to detect counter-mining.— CAMERA PRESS LTD.

defunct Germans would now be alive. And this was the way of it.

The presence of David in such an unhealthy locality as Flanders was entirely due to his regrettable lack of distinction between *meum* and *tuum*. Exactly what occurred is immaterial, but deciding that the evils he knew of in the shape of prison were probably worse than the evils he did not know of, in the shape of the Hun, our friend managed to evade the too pressing attentions of the police, and in due course found himself across the water in one of the new formed Tunnelling Companies. These companies are composed almost entirely of those who from their earliest infancy have been reared in the atmosphere of moles rather than in the atmosphere of men, and have as their work out here the great game of mining and countermining. Early in the proceedings it became apparent to those whose duty and privilege it was to command David Jones that his affection for woolly bears, pip-squeaks, crumps, Marias, and others of the great *genus obus* was not of that type which passeth the love of women. It is even rumoured that on one occasion, in a wood behind the line which was receiving attention from the Hun, and in which lay our hero's temporary abode, he made a voluntary confession of several real and imaginary misdeeds of his early youth in the hope of being sent back to prison and safety. Which is all by the way.

In the course of time, however, the Tunnelling Company was called upon to justify its existence – to become again as moles and not men, to gasp and sweat in the bowels of the earth – and thus the wood where they had been knew them no more. In front of our line, poked out a little from the German lines, there lay a semicircular redoubt. It was strong, very strong, as many officers in many regiments of foot will confirm. The ground in front of it bore eloquent testimony to frequent unsuccessful attempts to dislodge the enemy. Gunners had gunned it preparatory to assaults, gunners had gunned it all day and every day for many days, but so far in vain. Always were the infantry met with the same deadly cross machine-gun fire did they set foot over our parapet. Wherefore, having failed to subdue it from the air, and over the ground, they sent for the miners and told them to try from underneath. And thus it was that David Jones came again to his natural element.

Now I venture to think that of that natural element comparatively little is known by those who remain in the island over the water. The charge of cavalry, the thunder of guns, the grim infantry attack through the swirling mists of dawn, these can be visualized, can be imagined. Pictures by artists, quite a small percentage of which are more or less accurate, give to those who have never seen the dread drama of war a tolerably accurate impression of what happens. But of David Jones's natural element, of that work which goes on day and night, ceaselessly, burrowing under the ground nearer, ever nearer, the goal, there are no pictures to draw. And so before I come to tell of what my ruffian miner did under the earth in the place where the infantry had charged so often in vain, and of the German engineer officer who was discovered with part of his helmet forced into his brain and his head split asunder, I would digress for a space, and try to the best of my ability to paint that setting in which the human moles live and move and have their being.

I would take those who may care to follow me to the front-line trenches, where at a certain place – a sap head, perchance, or a Johnson hole just behind, or even in the trench itself – a deep, shored-up shaft has been sunk. From the front nothing is visible, and, by suitable screening, the inquisitive ones who fly overhead are prevented from seeing anything to cheer them up and make them excited. At the bottom of the shaft two men are sitting shovelling a heap of loose earth into buckets. Each bucket as it is filled is hoisted up on a rope working on a pulley – only to be lowered again empty when the earth has been tipped into some convenient shell hole, screened from the sight of the gentlemen opposite. If seen, the steady exodus of earth from a trench at one point is apt to give the Hun furiously to think – always an unwise proceeding. In front of the two men is a low black hole from which at regular intervals there comes a man, stripped to the waist, glistening with sweat, pushing a small trolley on leathered wheels. While the two men silently tip up the trolley and empty out the earth, he stands blinking for a moment at the patch of blue sky, only to disappear into the low, black hole, his trolley empty. Everything is silent; there is no hurry. Perhaps the occasional zip of a bullet, a lazy crump of a shell down the line; that is all, that and the low, black hole – ominous, sinister, the entrance to the mine.

And now mind your head; let us follow the man with the empty trolley. From far ahead comes the muffled thud of a pick, and behind one the light of day is streaming through the opening of the gallery. Bent almost double, one creeps forward, guiding oneself by one's hands as they touch walls that feel dank and cold. Then a turning, and utter, absolute darkness, until far ahead a faint light appears, the light at the front face of the mine. Another man pushing a full trolley squeezes past you, his body gleaming faintly white in the darkness, while steadily, without cessation, by the light of an electric lamp, the man on the front face goes on picking, picking, his body glistening as if it had been dipped in oil. When he is tired, another takes his place; there is no pause. Each yard as it is taken out is shored up with mine cases and sheeting, otherwise the whole thing may collapse on your head.

As you go on, your hands against the sides, you will find possibly an opening on one side or the other – the opening of another gallery, a gallery with a T head at the end, all finished. No earth is being carted from here, there is for the time no one in it; it is a listening gallery, and with the listening gallery and all it stands for we come to grips with the real drama of mining. Were it merely the mechanical removal of earth, the mechanical making of a tunnel from one place to another, it would perhaps be a safer occupation, but just as inspiring to write about as a new cure for corns. Moreover, it was from a listening gallery that David Jones – still, all in good time.

Mining, like most games, is one at which two can play, and it is not a matter of great surprise that neither side will allow the other one to play unmolested. Therefore, where there is mining there also is countermining, and the two operations are not exactly the same. For while mining is essentially an offensive act designed to blow up a portion of the enemy's trenches and form a crater in which men may shelter, countermining is essentially a defensive act designed merely to wreck the advancing mine. Thus both sides may at the same time be running out a mine towards the opposite trenches, and also a countermine in another part of the line to meet the hostile mine. Moreover, in a mine the charge is large, to effect as much damage as possible; in a countermine the charge is small, in order not to make too large a crater in which the enemy may unscrupulously take up his abode. All of which is essential for the proper understanding of David Jones – his act.

At periods, therefore, during the twenty-four hours all work in the mine is suspended. The muffled tapping of the pick ceases, and silence as of the grave reigns in the underground world. And during this period in each of the listening galleries skilled men stand with their ears glued to the earth, and some with instruments of which I may not speak, and listen. There under the earth, with their dead lying above them, in that No Man's Land between the trenches, with ears strained in the silence, a silence that can be felt, they listen for that dread noise, the muffled tap-tap of the enemy's miners countermining towards them. Sometimes the mine goes through without any countermine at all – more often not. Frequently the countermine is exploded too soon, or the direction is wrong and no damage is done, but sometimes it is otherwise. Sometimes there will be a dull, rumbling explosion – a few mine cases will fly upwards from the centre of the ground between the trenches, perhaps a boot or a head, but nothing more. And the miners will mine no more. The countermine has been successful.

But the estimation of distance and direction under the ground by listening to the muffled tap of the other man is a tricky business, and depends on many things. A fissure in the right direction, and it will sound close to, when in reality it is far away; an impervious strata across your front, and it will sound afar off, when in reality it is near.

Which all goes to show that it is a game of chance. But I would ask the armchair critic, the man in the street, if he have a spark of imagination, to transport himself to a mine where there is yet ten yards to go. Whenever for a space the moles stop, and the underworld silence settles like a pall, they hear the tap-tap of the other workers' ghostly fingers coming out to meet them. And then the tap-tap ceases. Have the others gone in the wrong direction, bearing away from them, or are they close to, three or four feet away even now charging the head of their countermine with explosive? Shall they go on, for time is precious, and finish that ten yards, or shall they stop awhile and see if they fire their countermine? Is it safe to do another two yards before they stop, or is it even now too late? Is that great tearing explosion coming at once, in the next second, or isn't it coming at all? And all the time those glistening, sweating men carry on – pick, pick, pick. It is for the officer in charge to decide, and until then . . .

Now, I don't for a moment think that David Jones regarded the matter at all in that light. An overmastering relief at being in a place where whizz-bangs cease from troubling and pip-squeaks are at rest drove out all lesser thoughts. When it happened he was as nearly contented as he was capable of being. The mine was ready to fire. Its head was well under the centre of the German redoubt, and all the morning slabs of gun-cotton had been carried up to the head. With loving care the electric leads had been taken up, the detonator fixed up – everything was ready. The earth to damp the charge, so laboriously carted out, had been brought back again, to prevent the force of the explosion blowing down the gallery instead of going upwards. And to the casual observer it seemed that the gallery ended merely in a solid wall of earth, into which vanished two harmless-looking black leads.

Now, the mine was going to be fired at seven o'clock in the evening. One does not prepare with great trouble an elaborate affair of that sort and then loose it off at any old time. All the infantry were warned – the gunners were warned – staff officers at discreet distances buzzed like bluebottles. As soon as it went off the infantry were to rush the redoubt, the gunners were to shell behind to prevent the counter-attack, and the staff were to have dinner. Which was all very right and proper.

The only one of these details which interested David was the hour at which the mine was to go off. Until that time he had fully made up his mind that the T head listening gallery, where he was comfortably smoking on a pile of sandbags, was a very much more desirable place than the trench up above, where, at or about the hour of five-thirty, the Hun was wont to hate with shells of great violence coming from a direction which almost enfiladed the trench. He recalled with distinct aversion the man next him the previous evening who had stopped a large piece of shell with his head.

At the same time he had no intention of remaining in the T head when the mine went off. Six-thirty struck him as a good and propitious moment to take his departure to the dangers of the upper air. David Jones was not a man to take any risk that could be avoided, and the mere fact that everyone had been ordered out of the mine had no bearing on the subject whatever. Like his personal courage, his sense of discipline was nil.

And so in the dark silence of the mine gallery, lying at ease on sandbags, with no horrible whistlings overhead, David Jones settled himself to rest and ruminate, and in the fulness of time he slept.

Now the mining operations had gone without a hitch. Apparently the Hun had no idea that his privacy was going to be invaded, and no sounds of countermining had been heard. Once, very faint it the distance, a tapping had been heard about three days after they had started. Since then it had not been repeated, and the officer in charge was not to be blamed for thinking that he had the show to himself. Nevertheless it is an undoubted fact that the thing which woke David Jones was a large piece of earth falling on his face, and a light shining through the face of the listening gallery. The next moment he heard a muttered ejaculation in a language he did not know, and great masses of earth rained down on his face while the light was extinguished. His training as a miner enabled him to see in a moment what had happened. That part of his mind worked instinctively. A German gallery had opened into their listening gallery. Some strata of soil had rendered it almost soundless, and his sleep during the last two hours had prevented him hearing the approach through the final two feet. All that he grasped in a flash; but what was far more to the point, he realized that in about two seconds he would be face to face with a horrible Hun, a prospect which turned him cold with horror. Had he been capable of getting up, had his legs been capable of overcoming his terror, there is but little doubt that he would have fled to the safety of the open air. After all, a problematic shell is better than an encounter with a large and brutal man underground.

But before he could move, a head and shoulders followed by a body came through the opening and fell almost on top of him. A torch was cautiously flashed, and by its light the trembling David saw a large and brutal-looking man peering round. Then the man moved forward. Evidently he had seen that he was in a gallery off the main one, and had failed to see our hero sheltering behind the sandbags. For a long while there was silence. David could hear the German's heavy breathing, as he stood a few feet from him just where the main gallery crossed the entrance to the T head. He realized that he was afraid to flash his torch until he was quite certain there was no one about.

But now David's mind was moving with feverish activity. So far he had escaped detection – but supposing more of these terrible beings came. Supposing this one came back and did not overlook him again. The thought nerved him to action. Cautiously, without a sound he raised himself from behind the pile of sandbags and crept to the spot where the T head left the short gallery that connected it to the main one, and there he stood in the inky darkness with the German a few feet in front of him. His plan was to make a dash for safety when the German started to explore the main gallery.

It seemed an eternity – in reality it was about half a minute – before the light was again flashed cautiously into the darkness. It cast round in a circle and then came to a halt. He heard the sharp intake of the German's breath, and saw the light fixed on the two black leads. Then things moved quickly.

The German laid down his pick, and fumbled in his pocket for his wire-cutters. Those leads told their story plain for all to read. Again, in a flash, the dangers of his position struck David. This accursed Hun would cut the leads and then return, and run straight into him. He wouldn't bother to explore the gallery further. He would merely murder him, and pass on. A horrible thought.

With infinite caution he reached for the pick. The German was muttering to himself and trying to detach his wire-cutters from his belt. At last he had them free, and, flashing his torch once again, stooped forward to cut the lead. And as he did so with a grunt, David Jones struck – struck at the centre of the head outlined in the circle of light. There was a dreadful half-choked cry and – silence.

Two minutes later David Jones was in the trench looking fearfully over his shoulder as if expecting pursuit. The idea of warning the officer in charge that a German gallery had struck through into theirs never even entered his head. It was a matter of complete indifference to him if another Hun came in and cut the wire, so long as he wasn't on hand to be cut too. So it was fortunate perhaps that David had overslept himself, as one minute after his arrival in the upper earth there was a deafening thunderous roar. A great mass of earth, roots, wood, and other fragments flew upwards and then came raining down again. The infantry were across in a flash – the curtain of shrapnel descended – and the staff had dinner.

There were two things that no one ever cleared up satisfactorily. One was the presence of a miner's pick, of a pattern different to that in use in the British Army, in the tool dump of a certain Tunnelling Company. But it was a very small thing, and no one worried.

The other was the presence of a German Engineer Officer in the mine shaft with his helmet, or part of it, in his brain. Various opinions were given by various people; but as they were all wrong, they don't matter. Anyway, the mine had been most successful – and everybody shook hands with everybody.

All, that is, except David Jones, who was undergoing Field Punishment Number One for stealing the emergency rum ration and getting drunk on it.

Which is really rather humorous when you come to think of it.

From: *The Lieutenant And Others.*

'*SAPPER*' (Lieutenant-Colonel H. C. McNeile) was born in 1888. A writer of popular adventure stories and creator of the *Bulldog Drummond* series, he was educated at Cheltenham College and the Royal Military Academy, Woolwich. He served with the Royal Engineers as a professional soldier from 1907, and began writing during the First World War. He died in 1937.

R.F.A.

A TRADE REPORT ONLY

C E Montague

1

No one has said what was wrong with The Garden, nor even why it was called by that name : whether because it had apples in it, and also a devil, like Eden; or after Gethsemane and the agonies there; or, again, from Proserpine's garden, because of the hush filling the foreground. All the air near you seemed like so much held breath, with the long rumble of far-away guns stretching out beyond it like some dreamful line of low hills in the distance of a landscape.

The rest of the Western Front has been well written up – much too well. The Garden alone – the Holy Terror, as some of the men used to call it – has not. It is under some sort of taboo. I think I know why. If you never were in the line there before the smash came and made it like everywhere else, you could not know how it would

An RFA soldier with a dog, walking across the shell-torn streets of Ypres on 27 September 1917.—CAMERA PRESS LTD.

work on the nerves when it was still its own elfish self. And if you were there and did know, then you knew also that it was no good to try to tell people. They only said, 'Oh, so you all had the wind up?' We had. But who could say why? How is a horse to say what it is that bedevils one empty place more than another? He has to prick up his ears when he gets there. Then he starts sweating. That's all he knows, and it was the same story with us in The Garden. All I can do is to tell you, just roughly, the make of the place, the way that the few honest solids and liquids were fixed that came into it. They were the least part of it, really.

It was only an orchard, to look at; all ancient apple-trees, dead straight in the stem, with fat, wet grass underneath, a little unhealthy in colour for want of more sun. Six feet above ground the lowest apple boughs all struck out level, and kept so; some beasts, gone in our time, must have eaten every leaf that tried to grow lower. So the under side of the boughs made a sort of flat awning or roof. We called the layer of air between it and the ground The Six-foot Seam, as we were mostly miners. The light in this seam always appeared to have had something done to it: sifted through branches, refracted, messed about somehow, it was not at all the stuff you wanted just at that time. You see the like of it in an eclipse, when the sun gives a queer wink at the earth round the edge of a black mask. Very nice, too, in its place; but the war itself was quite enough out of the common – falling skies all over the place, and half your dead certainties shaken.

We and the Germans were both in The Garden, and knew it. But nobody showed. Everywhere else on the front somebody showed up at last; somebody fired. But here nothing was seen or heard, ever. You found you were whispering and walking on tiptoe, expecting you didn't know what. Have you been in a great crypt at twilight under a church, nothing round you but endless thin pillars, holding up a low roof? Suppose there's a wolf at the far end of the crypt and you alone at the other, staring and staring into the thick of the pillars, and wondering, wondering – round which of the pillars will that grey nose come rubbing?

Why not smash up the silly old spell, you may say – let a good yell, loose a shot, do any sane thing to break out? That's what I said till we got there. Our unit took over the place from the French. A French platoon sergeant, my opposite number, showed me the quarters and posts and the like, and I asked the usual question, 'How's the old Boche?'

'*Mais assez gentil,*' he pattered. That Gaul was not waiting to chat. While he showed me the bomb-store, he muttered something low, hurried, and blurred – '*Le bon Dieu Boche,*' I think it was, had created the orchard. The Germans themselves were '*bons bourgeois*' enough, for all he had seen or heard of them – 'Not a shot in three weeks. *Seulement*' – he grinned, half-shamefaced and half-confidential, as sergeant to sergeant – '*ne faut pas les embêter*'.

I knew all about that. French sergeants were always like that: dervishes in a fight when it came, but dead set, at all other times, on living *paisiblement*, smoking their pipes. *Paisiblement* – they love the very feel of the word in their mouths. Our men were no warrior race, but they all hugged the belief that they really were marksmen, not yet found out by the world. They would be shooting all night at clods, at tops of posts, at anything that might pass for a head. Oh, I knew. Or I thought so.

But no. Not a shot all the night. Nor on any other night either. We were just sucked into the hush of The Garden the way your voice drops in a church – when you go in at the door you become part of the system. I tried to think why. Did nobody fire just because in that place it was so easy for anybody to kill? No trench could be dug; it would have filled in an hour with water filtering through from the full stream flanking The Garden. Sentries stood out among the fruit trees, behind little breastworks of sods, like the things you use to shoot grouse. These screens were merely a form; they would scarcely have slowed down a bullet. They were not defences, only symbols of things that were real elsewhere. Everything else in the place was on queer terms with reality; so were they.

II

Our first event was the shriek. It was absolutely detached, unrelated to anything seen or heard before or soon after, just like the sudden fall of a great tree on a windless day. At three o'clock on a late autumn morning, a calm moonless night, the depths of The Garden in front of our posts yielded a long wailing scream. I was making a round of our posts at the time, and the scream made me think of a kind of dream I had had twice or thrice; not a story dream, but a portrait dream; just a vivid rending vision of the face of some friend with a look on it that made me feel the brute I must have been to have never seen how he or she had suffered, and how little I had known or tried to know. I could not have fancied before that one yell could tell such a lot about anyone. Where it came from there must be some kind of hell going on that went beyond all the hells now in the books, like one of the stars that are still out of sight because the world has not lived long enough to give time for the first ray of light from their blaze to come through to our eyes.

I found the sentries jumpy. 'What is it, sergeant?' one of them almost demanded of me, as if I were the fellow in charge of the devils. 'There's no one on earth,' he said, 'could live in that misery.'

Toomey himself, the red-headed gamekeeper out of the County Fermanagh, betrayed some perturbation. He hinted that 'Them wans' were in it. 'Who?' I asked. 'Ach, the Good People,' he said, with a trace of reluctance. Then I remembered, from old days at school, that the Greeks, too, had been careful; they called their Furies 'The Well-disposed Ladies'.

All the rest of the night there was not a sound but the owls. The sunless day that followed was quiet till 2.30 p.m., when the Hellhound appeared. He came trotting briskly out of the orchard, rounding stem after stem of the fruit trees, leapt our little pretence of barbed wire, and made straight for Toomey, then on guard, as any dog would. It was a young male black-and-tan. It adored

Toomey till three, when he was relieved. Then it came capering around him in ecstasy, back to the big living cellar, a hundred yards in the rear. At the door it heard voices within and let down its tail, ready to plead lowliness and contrition before any tribunal less divine than Toomey.

The men, or most of them, were not obtrusively divine just then. They were out to take anything ill that might come. All the hushed days had first drawn their nerves tight, and then the scream had cut some of them. All bawled or squeaked in the cellar, to try to feel natural after the furtive business outside.

'Gawd a'mighty!' Looker shrilled at the entry of Toomey, 'if Fritz ain't sold 'im a pup!'

Jeers flew from all parts of the smoky half-darkness. 'Where's licence, Toomey?'

'Sure 'e's clean in th' 'ouse?'

' 'Tain't no Dogs' 'Ome 'ere. Over the way!'

Corporal Mullen, the ever-friendly, said to Toomey, more mildly, 'Wot? Goin' soft?'

'A daycent dog, corp,' said Toomey. 'He's bruk wi' the Kaiser. An' I'll engage he's through the distemper. Like as not he'll be an Alsatian.' Toomey retailed these commendations slowly, with pauses between, to let them sink in.

'What'll you feed him?' asked Mullen, inspecting the points of the beast with charity.

'Feed 'im!' Looker squealed. 'Feed 'im into th' incinerator!'

Toomey turned on him. 'Aye, an' be et be the rats!'

'Fat lot o' talk about rats,' growled Brunt, the White Hope, the company's only prize-fighter. 'Tha'd think rats were struttin' down fairway, shovin' folk off duck-board.'

'Ah!' Looker agreed. 'An' roostin' up yer armpit.'

'Thot's reet,' said Brunt.

'I'll bet 'arf a dollar,' said Looker, eyeing the Hellhound malignantly, 'the 'Uns 'ave loaded him up with plague fleas. Sent 'im acrorse. Wiv instructions.'

Toomey protested. 'Can't ye see the dog has been hit, ye blind man?' In fact, the immigrant kept his tail licking expressively under his belly except when it lifted under the sunshine of Toomey's regard.

Brunt rumbled out slow gloomy prophecies from the gloom of his corner. ' 'E'll be tearin' 'imself t'bits wi' t'mange in a fortneet. Rat for breakfas', rat for dinner, rat for tea; bit o' rat las' thing at neet, 'fore 'e'll stretch down to 't.'

'An' that's the first sinse ye've talked,' Toomey conceded. 'A rotten diet-sheet is ut. An' dirt! An' no kennel the time the roof'll start drippin'. A dog's life for a man, an' God knows what for a dog.'

We felt the force of that. We all had dogs at home. The Hell-hound perhaps felt our ruth in the air like a rise of temperature, for at this point he made a couple of revolutions on his wheel base, to get the pampas grass of his imagination comfortable about him, and then collapsed in a curve and lay at rest with his nose to the ground and two soft enigmatic gleams from his eyes raking the twilight recesses of our dwelling. For the moment he was relieved of the post of nucleus-in-chief for the vapours of fractiousness to condense upon.

He had a distinguished successor. The company sergeant-major, no less, came round about five minutes after with 'word from the colonel'. Some mischief, all our hearts told us at once. They were right too. The Corps had sent word – just what it would, we inwardly groaned. The Corps had sent word that G.H.Q. – Old G.H.Q.! At it again! we savagely thought. We knew what was coming. Yes G.H.Q. wanted to know what German unit was opposite to us. That meant a raid, of course. The colonel couldn't help it. Like all sane men below brigade staffs, he hated raids. But orders were orders. He did all he could. He sent word that if anyone brought in a German, dead or alive, on his own, by this time to-morrow, he, the colonel, would give him a fiver. Of course nobody could, but it was an offer, meant decently.

Darkness and gnashing of teeth, grunts and snarls of disgust, filled the cellar the moment the C.S.M. had departed. 'Gawd 'elp us!' 'A ride! In The Gawden!' ' 'Oo says Gawd made gawdens?' 'Ow! Everythink in The Gawden is lovely!' 'Come into The Gawden, Maud!' You see, the wit of most of us was not a weapon of precision. Looker came nearest, perhaps, to the point. 'As if we 'ad a chawnce,' he said, 'to gow aht rattin' Germans, wiv a sack!'

'We gotten dog for't ahl reet,' said Brunt. This was the only audible trace of good humour. Toomey looked at Brunt quickly.

Toomey was destined to trouble that afternoon; one thing came after another. At 3.25 I sent him and Brunt, with a clean sack apiece, to the sergeant-major's dug-out for the rations. They came back in ten minutes. As Toomey gave me his sack, I feared that I saw a thin train of mixed black and white dust trending across the powdered mortar floor to the door. Then I saw Looker, rage in his face, take a candle and follow this trail, stooping down, and once tasting the stuff on a wet finger-tip.

And then the third storm burst. 'Christ!' Looker yelled. 'If 'e ain't put the tea in the sack wiv a 'ole in it!'

We all knew that leak in a bottom corner of that special sack as we knew every very small thing in our life of small things – the cracked dixie-lid, the brazier's short leg, the way that Mynns had of clearing his throat, and Brunt of working his jaws before spitting. Of course, the sack was all right for loaves and the tinned stuff. But tea! – loose tea mixed with powdered sugar! It was like loading a patent seed-sowing machine with your fortune in gold-dust. There was a general groan of 'God help us!' with extras. In this report I leave out, all along, a great many extras. Print and paper are dear.

Looker was past swearing. 'Plyin' a piper-chise!' he ejaculated with venom. 'All owver Frawnce! Wiv our grub!'

Toomey was sorely distressed. He, deep in whose heart was lodged the darling vision of Toomey the managing head, the contriver, the 'oul lad that was in ut', had bungled a job fit for babes. 'Ah, then, who could be givin' his mind to the tea,' he almost moaned, 'an' he with a grand thought in ut?'

At any other time and place the platoon would have settled down, purring, under those words. 'A grand thought', 'a great idaya' – when Toomey in happier days had owned to being in labour with one of these heirs of his invention, some uncovenanted mercy had nearly always accrued before long to his friends – a stew of young rabbits, two brace of fat pheasants, once a mighty wild goose. The tactician, we understood in a general way, had 'put the comether upon' them. Now even those delicious memories were turned to gall. 'Always the sime!' Looker snarled at the fallen worker of wonders. 'Always the sime! Ye cawn't 'ave a bit o' wire sived up for pipe-cleanin' without 'e'll loan it off yer to go snarin' 'ares.' Looker paused for a moment, gathering all the resources of wrath, and then he swiftly scaled the high top-gallant of ungraciousness: ' 'E wiv the 'ole platoon workin' awye for 'im, pluckin' pawtridge an' snipes, the 'ole wye up from the sea! Top end o' Frawnce is all a muck o' feathers wiv 'im!'

All were good men; Looker, like Toomey, a very good man. It was only their nerves that had gone, and the jolly power of gay and easy relentment after a jar. However they tried, they could not cease yapping. I went out for a drink of clean air. If you are to go on loving mankind, you must take a rest from it sometimes. As I went up the steps from the cellar the rasping jangle from below did not cease; it only sank on my ears as I went. 'Ow, give us 'Owm Rule for England, Gord's sike!' 'Sye there ain't no towds in Irelan', do they?' 'Looker, I've tould you I'm sorry, an' – ' 'Garn, both on yer! Ol' gas-projectors!' 'Begob, if ye want an eye knocked from ye then – !' I was going back, but then I heard Corporal Mullen, paternal and firm, like Neptune rebuking the winds. 'Now, then, we don't none of us want to go losing our heads about nothing.' No need to trouble. Mullen would see to the children.

III

I went east, into The Garden. Ungathered apples were going to loss on its trees. I stood looking at one of them for a time, and then it suddenly detached itself and fell to the ground with a little thud and a splash of squashed brown rottenness, as if my eye had plucked it. After that sound the stillness set in again: stillness of autumn, stillness of vigilant fear, and now the stillness of oncoming evening, the nun, to make it more cloistral. No silence so deep but that it can be deepened! As minutes passed, infinitesimal whispers – I think from mere wisps of eddies, twisting round snags in the stream – began to lift into hearing. Deepening silence is only the rise into clearness, of this or that more confidential utterance.

I must have been sucking that confidence in for a good twenty minutes before I turned with a start. I had to, I did not know why. It seemed as if some sense, which I did not know I had got, told me that someone was stealing up behind me. No one there; nothing but Arras, the vacuous city, indistinct among her motionless trees. She always seemed to be listening and frightened. It was as if the haggard creature had stirred.

I looked to my front again, rather ashamed. Was I losing hold too? I wondered as I gazed level out into the Seam and watched the mist deepening. Each evening that autumn, a quilt of very white mist would come out of the soaked soil of The Garden, lay itself out, flat and dense, but shallow at first, over the grass, and then deepen upward as twilight advanced, first submerging the tips of the grass and the purple snake-headed flowers; and then thickening steadily up till the whole Six-foot Seam was packed with milky opaqueness.

Sixty yards out from our front a heron was standing, immobilized, in the stream, staring down – for a last bit of fishing no doubt. As I watched him, his long head came suddenly round and half up. He listened. He stood like that, warily, for a minute, then seemed to decide it was no place for him, hoisted himself off the ground, and winged slowly away with great flaps. I felt cold, and thought, 'What a time I've been loafing round here!' But I found it was four o'clock only. I thought I would go on and visit my sentries, the three-o'clock men who would come off duty at five. It would warm me; and one or two of the young ones were apt to be creepy about sundown.

Schofield, the lad in one of our most advanced posts, was waist-deep in the mist when I reached him.

'Owt, boy?' I whispered. He was a North-country man.

'Nowt, sergeant,' he answered, 'barrin' – ' He checked. He

was one of the stout ones you couldn't trust to yell out for help if the Devil were at them.

'What's wrong?' I asked pretty sharply.

'Nobbut t'way,' he said slowly, 'they deucks doan't seem t'be gettin' down to it to-neet.' My eye followed his through the boughs to the pallid sky. A flight of wild-duck were whirling and counter-whirling aloft in some odd *pas d'inquiétude*. Yes; no doubt our own ducks that had come during the war, with the herons and snipe, to live in The Garden, the untrodden marsh where, between the two lines of rifles never unloaded, no shot was ever heard and snipe were safe from all snipers. A good lad, Schofield; he took a lot of notice of things. But what possessed the creatures? What terror infested their quarters tonight?

I looked Schofield over. He was as near to dead white as a tanned man can come – that is, a bad yellow. But he could be left. A man that keeps on taking notice of things he can see, instead of imagining ones that he can't, is a match for the terror that walketh by twilight. I stole on to our most advanced post of all. There I was not so sure of my man. He was Mynns. We call him Billy Wisdom, because he was a schoolmaster in civil life – some council school at Hoggerston. 'What cheer, Billy?' I whispered. 'Anything to report?'

The mist was armpit deep on him now, but the air quite clear above that; so that from three feet off I saw his head and shoulders well, and his bayonet; nothing else at all. He did not turn when I spoke, nor unfix his eyes from the point he had got them set on, in front of his post and a little below their own level. 'All – quiet – and – correct – sergeant,' he said, as if each word were a full load and had to be hauled by itself. I had once seen a man drop his rifle and bolt back overland from his post, to trial and execution and anything rather than that everlasting wait for a bayonet's point to come lunging up out of thick mist in front and a little below him, into the gullet, under the chin. Billy was near bolting-point, I could tell by more senses than one. He was losing hold on one bodily function after another, but still hanging on hard to something, some grip of the spirit that held from second to second, after muscle had mutinied and nerve was gone.

He had hardly spoken before a new torment wrung him. The whole landscape suddenly gave a quick shiver. The single poplar, down the stream, just perceptibly shuddered and rustled, and then was dead still again. A bed of rushes, nearer us, swayed for an instant, and stood taut again. Absurd, you will say. And, of course, it was only a faint breath of wind, the only stir in the air all that day. But you were not there. So you cannot feel how the cursed place had tried to shake itself free of its curse, and had failed and fallen rigid again, dreeing its weird, and poor Billy with it. His hold on his tongue was what he lost now. He began to wail under his breath, 'Christ, pity me! Oh, suffering Christ, pity me!' He was still staring hard to his front, but I had got a hand ready to grab at his belt when, from somewhere out in the mist before us, there came, short and crisp, the crack of a dead branch heavily trodden upon.

Billy was better that instant. Better an audible enemy, one with a body, one that could trample on twigs, than that vague infestation of life with impalpable sinisterness. Billy turned with a grin – ghastly enough, but a grin.

'Hold your fire,' I said in his ear, 'till I order.' I made certain dispositions of bombs on a little shelf. Then we waited, listening, second by second. I think both our ears must have flicked like a mule's. But the marvel came in at the eye. We both saw the vision at just the same instant. It was some fifty yards from us, straight to our front. It sat on the top of the mist as though mist were ice and would bear. It was a dog, of the very same breed as the Hell-hound, sitting upright like one of the beasts that support coats-of-arms; all proper too, as the heralds would say, with the black and tan hues as in life. The image gazed at us fixedly. How long? Say, twenty seconds. Then it about-turned without any visible use of its limbs, and receded some ten or twelve yards, still sitting up and now rhythmically rising and falling as though the mist it rode upon were undulating. Then it clean vanished. I thought it sank, as if the mist had ceased to bear. Billy thought the beast just melted into the air radially, all round, as rings made of smoke do.

You know the crazy coolness, a sort of false presence of mind, that will come in and fool you a little bit further at these moments of staggering dislocation of cause and effect. One of these waves of mad rationalism broke on me now. I turned quickly round to detect the cinema lantern behind us which must have projected the dog's moving figure upon the white sheet of mist. None there, of course. Only the terrified city, still there, aghast, with held breath.

Then all my anchors gave together. I was adrift; there was nothing left certain. I thought, 'What if all we are sure of be just a mistake, and our sureness about it conceit, and we no better than puppies ourselves to wonder that dogs should be taking their ease in mid-air and an empty orchard be shrieking?' While I was drifting, I happened to notice the sleepy old grumble of guns from the rest of the front, and I envied those places. Sane, normal places; happy all who were there; only their earthworks were crumbling, not the last few certainties that we men think we have got hold of.

All this, of course, had to go on in my own mind behind a shut face. For Billy was one of the nerve specialists; he might get a V.C., or be shot in a walled yard at dawn, according to how he was handled. So I was pulling my wits together a little, to dish out some patter fit for his case – you know: the 'bright, breezy, brotherly' bilge – when the next marvel came. A sound this time – a voice, too; no shriek, not even loud, but tranquil, articulate, slow, and so distant that only the deathly stillness which gave high relief to every bubble that burst with a plop, out in the marsh, could bring the words to us at all. 'Has annywan here lost a dog? Annywan lost a good dog? Hoond? Goot Hoond? Annywan lost a goot hoond?'

You never can tell how things will take you. I swear I was right out of that hellish place for a minute or more, alive and free and back at home among the lost delights of Epsom Downs, between the races; the dear old smelly crowd all over the course, and the merchant who carries a tray crying, ' 'Oo'll 'ave a good cigar, gents? Two pence! 'Oo wants a good cigar? Two pence! 'Oo says a good smoke?' And the sun shining good on all the bookies and crooks by the rails, the just and the unjust, all jolly and natural. Better than Lear's blasted heath and your mind running down!

You could see the relief settle on Mynns like oil going on to a burn on your hand. Have you seen an easy death in bed? – the yielding sigh of peace and the sinking inwards, the weary job over? It was like that. He breathed 'That Irish swine!' in a voice that made it a blessing. I felt the same, but more uneasily. One of my best was out there in the wide world, having God knew what truck with the enemy. Any Brass Hat that came loafing round might think, in his blinded soul, that Toomey was fraternizing; whereas Toomey was dead or prisoner by now, or as good, unless delivered by some miracle of gumption surpassing all his previous practices against the brute creation. We could do nothing, could not even guess where he was in the fog. It had risen right up to the boughs; the whole Seam was packed with it, tight. No one but he who had put his head into the mouth of the tiger could pull it out now.

We listened on, with pricked ears. Voices we certainly heard; yes, more than one; but not a word clear. And voices were not what I harked for – it was for the shot that would be the finish of Toomey. I remembered during the next twenty minutes quite a lot of good points about Toomey. I found that I had never had a sulky word from him, for one. At the end of the twenty minutes the voices finally stopped. But no shot came. A prisoner, then?

The next ten minutes were bad. Towards the end of the two hours for which they lasted I could have fancied the spook symptoms were starting again. For out of the mist before us there came something that was not seen, or heard, or felt; no one sense could fasten upon it; only a mystic consciousness came of some approaching displacement of the fog. The blind, I believe, feel the same when they come near a lamp-post. Slowly this undefined source of impressions drew near, from out the uncharted spaces beyond, to the frontiers of hearing and sight, slipped across them and took form, at first as the queerest tangle of two sets of limbs, and then as Toomey, bearing on one shoulder a large corpse, already stiff, clothed in field-grey.

IV

'May I come in, sergeant?' said Toomey, 'an' bring me sheaves wid me?' The pride of 'cuteness shone from his eyes like a lamp through the fog; his voice had the urbanely affected humility of the consciously great.

'You may,' said I, 'if you've given nothing away.'

'I have not,' said he. 'I'm an importer entirely. Me exports are nil.' He rounded the flank of the breastwork and laid the body tenderly down, as a collector would handle a Strad. 'There wasn't the means of an identification about me. Me shoulder titles, me badge, me pay-book, me small-book, me disc, an' me howl correspondence – I left all beyant in the cellar. They'd not have got value that tuk me.' Toomey's face was all one wink. To value himself on his courage would never enter his head. It was the sense of the giant intellect within that filled him with triumph.

I inspected the bulging eyes of the dead. 'Did you strangle him sitting?' I asked.

'Not at all. Amn't I just after tradin' the dog for him?' Then, in the proper whisper, Toomey made his report:

'Ye'll remember the whillabalooin' there was at meself in the cellar. Leppin' they were, at the loss of the tea. The end of it was that "I'm goin' out now," said I, "to speak to a man," said I, "about a dog", an' I quitted the place, an' the dog with me, knockin' his nose against every lift of me heel. I'd a grand thought in me head, to make them whisht thinkin' bad of me. Very near where the lad Schofiel' is, I set out for Germ'ny, stoopin' low, to get all the use of the fog. Did you notus me, sergeant?'

'Breaking the firewood?' I said.

'Aye, I med sure that ye would. So I signalled.'

Now I perceived. Toomey went on. 'I knew, when I held up the dog on the palm of me hand, ye'd see where I was, an' where goin'. Then I wint on, deep into th' East. Their wire is nothin' at all; it's the very spit of our own. I halted among ut, and gev out a notus, in English an' German, keepin' well down in the fog to rejuce me losses. They didn't fire – ye'll have heard that. They sint for the man with the English. An', be the will o' God, he was the same man that belonged to the dog.'

' "Hans," says I, courcheous but firm, "the dog is well off where he is. Will you come to him quietly?"

'I can't jus' give ye his words, but the sinse of them only. "What are ye doin' at all," he says, "askin' a man to desert?"

'There was serious trouble in that fellow's voice. It med me ashamed. But I wint on, an' only put double strength in me temptin's. "Me colonel," I told him, "is offerin' five pounds for a prisoner. Come back with me now and ye'll have fifty francs for yourself when I get the reward. Think over ut well. Fifty francs down. There's a grand lot of spendin' in that. An' ye'll be wi' the dog." As I offered him each injucement, I lifted th' an'mal clear of the fog for two seconds or three, to keep the man famished wid longin'. You have to be crool in a war. Each time that I lowered the dog I lep' two paces north, under the fog, to be-divvil their aim if they fired.

' "Ach, to hell wi' your francs an' your pounds," says he in his ag'ny. "Give me the dog or I'll shoot. I see where you are."

' "I'm not there at all," says I, "an' the dog's in front of me bosom."

'Ye'll understan', sergeant,' Toomey said to me gravely, 'that last was a ruse. I'd not do the like o' that to a dog, anny more than yourself.

'The poor divvil schewed in his juice for a while, very quiet. Then he out with an offer. "Will ye take sivinty francs for the dog? It's the whole of me property. An' it only comes short be five francs of th' entire net profuts ye'd make on the fiver, an' I comin' with you."

' "I will not," says I, faint and low. It was tormint refusin' the cash.

' "Won't *annythin'* do ye," says he in despair, "but a live wan?"

' "Depinds," says I pensively, playin' me fish. I held up the dog for a second again, to keep his sowl workin'.

'He plunged, at the sight of the creature. "Couldn't ye do with a body?" he says very low.

' "Depinds," says I, marvellin' was ut a human sacrifice he was for makin', the like of the Druids, to get back the dog.

' "Not fourteen hours back," says he, "he died on us."

' "Was he wan of yourselves?" says I. "A nice fool I'd look if I came shankin' back from the fair wid a bit of the wrong unit."

' "He was," says he, "an' the best of us all." An' then he went on, wid me puttin' in just a word now and then, or a glimpse of the dog, to keep him desirous and gabbin'. There's no use in cheapenin' your wares. He let on how this fellow he spoke of had never joyed since they came to that place, an' gone mad at the finish wi' not gettin' his sleep without he'd be seein' Them Wans in a dream and hearin' the Banshies; the way he bruk out at three in the morning that day, apt to cut anny in two that would offer to hold him. "Here's out of it all," he appeared to have said; "I've lived through iv'ry room in hell, how long, O Lord, how long, but it's glory an' victory now," an' off an' away wid him West, through The Garden. "Ye'll not have seen him at all?" says me friend. We hadn't notussed, I told him. "We were right then," says he; "he'll have died on the way. For he let a scream in the night that a man couldn't give an' live after. If he'd fetched up at your end," says he, "you'd have known, for he was as brave as a lion."

' "A livin' dog's better," says I, "than anny dead lion. It's a Jew's bargain you're makin'. Where's the deceased?"

' "Pass me the dog," says he, "an I'll give you his route out from here to where he'll have dropped. It's his point of deparchure I stand at."

' "I'll come to ye there," says I, "an' ye'll give me his bearin's, an' when I've set eyes on me man I'll come back an' hand ye the dog, an' not sooner."

'He was spaichless a moment. "Come now," says I, from me lair in the fog, "wan of the two of us has to be trustful. I'll not let ye down."

' "Ye'll swear to come back?" says he in great anguish.

'I said, "Tubbe sure."

' "Come on with ye, then," he answered.

'I went stoopin' along to within six feet of his voice, the way ye'd swim under water, an' then I came to the surface. The clayey-white face that he had, an' the top of his body showed over a breastwork the moral of ours. An', be cripes, it was all right. The red figures were plain on his shoulder-strap – wan-eighty-six. Another breastwork the fellow to his was not thirty yards south. There was jus' the light left me to see that the sentry there was wan-eighty-six too. I'd inspicted the goods in bulk now, an' only had to see to me sample an' off home with it.'

Toomey looked benedictively down on the long stiff frame with its Iron Cross ribbon and red worsted '186'. 'An ould storm-throoper!' Toomey commendingly said. 'His friend gev me the line to him. Then he got anxious. "Ye'll bury him fair?" he said. "Is he a Prod'stant?" says I, "or a Cath'lic?" "A good Cath'lic," says he; "we're Bavarians here." "Good," says I, "I'll speak to Father Moloney meself." "An' ye'll come back," says he, "wi' the dog?" "I will not," says I, "I shall hand him ye now. Ye're a straight man not to ha' shot me before. Besides, ye're a Cath'lic?" So I passed him the an'mal and off on me journey. Not the least trouble at all, findin' the body. The birds were all pointin' to ut. They hated ut. Faith, but that fellow had seen the quare things!' Toomey looked down again at the monstrously staring eyes of his capture, bursting with agonies more fantastic, I thought, than any that stare from the bayoneted dead in a trench.

'The man wi' the dog,' Toomey said, 'may go the same road. His teeth are all knockin' together. A match for your own, Billy.' In trenches you did not pretend not to know all about one another, the best and the worst. In that screenless life friendship frankly condoled with weak nerves or an ugly face or black temper.

'Sergeant,' said Toomey, 'ye'll help me indent for the fiver? A smart drop of drink it'll be for the whole of the boys.'

I nodded. 'Bring him along,' I said, 'now.'

'Well, God ha' mercy on his sowl,' said Toomey, hoisting the load on to his back.

'And of all Christian souls, I pray God.' I did not say it. Only

Ophelia's echo, crossing my mind. How long would Mynns last? Till I could wangle his transfer to the divisional laundry or gaff?

I brought Toomey along to claim the fruit of his guile. We had to pass Schofield. He looked more at ease in his mind than before. I asked the routine question. 'All correct, sergeant,' he answered. 'Deucks is coom dahn. Birds is all stretchin' dahn to it, proper.'

Its own mephitic mock-peace was refilling The Garden. But no one can paint a miasma. Anyhow, I am not trying to. This is a trade report only.

From: *Fiery Particles.*

C. E. MONTAGUE, an Irish-born journalist, novelist, and critic, was born in January 1867, and educated at the City of London School and Balliol College, Oxford, where he took a First in Classics and a Second in *literae humaniores.* Joining the *Manchester Guardian* in 1890, he became chief assistant to the editor and proprietor, C. P. Scott, in 1898, and married Scott's daughter. On the outbreak of war in 1914, he dyed his grey hair brown and enlisted as a private with the Royal Fusiliers at the age of forty-seven. His health gave way after some months' active service on the Western Front and he was invalided home, but went out again in 1916 in the Intelligence Service. His bitter war novel *Disenchantment* was published in 1922, *Fiery Particles* in 1923. Montague, a skilled Alpinist, died in May 1928.

THE DEBRIS

Ernest Raymond

There is a farm near Proven behind Poperinghe, where how many battalions have rested, going up at full strength with their bayonets sharpened and their junior officers in privates' kit to take their part in the Salient, and how many have halted on their backward journey, thinking of friends who were in these rooms and barns when last they rested here, it might be possible for archives to show; and the exact number of voices, too, that must have echoed in the brick-paved rooms of its farmhouse, before going onward to be quieted in the mud, this might be worked out by an auditor with a genius for figures; but of all the myriad closeted emotions suffered there by these pilgrims – emotions that were never brought out from behind their curtains of laughter – it is forever beyond the arithmetic of man to make the tally. Doubtless the Flemish farmer and Madame his wife work there now; and to their honest peasant minds, hard

A postcard of officers posing for a group photograph to celebrate their passing a training course in England, 1916.

and dull, the impregnated walls whisper nothing; when after a laborious day they take their tired bodies to that room upstairs to sleep, their dreams, if they dream at all, are not troubled by the scenes which the room has witnessed; they know nothing of Captain Scrase and Lieutenant O'Grogan, and Colonel Tappiter and old Joe Wylie; nor of a shot that was fired here, years and years ago. And that smaller room which opens off this one, and whose door is probably always closed since it holds nothing but lumber and boxes, there Joe Wylie piled his kit and stood his rifle in a corner and cooked a meal for his officers. In the room just across the passage Scrase slept when he was under close arrest, and Tony by his side, as the officer in charge of him. This room itself where, as we conjecture, the farmer and his wife sleep today, was no more than their place of messing, for there was ample accommodation – only too ample – in the farmhouse and the barns and the tents beyond the midden for the 15th Royal West Essex when they came back from the battle of Passchendaele, not a hundred bayonets strong. Battalion Headquarters had the ground-floor rooms, and the arrested officer, and Tony his guardian, were lodged – one had almost said 'secreted' – in these rooms upstairs.

A late October day in Passchendaele's year; and Scrase stood staring out of the window at the level plain with its blown poplars, and at the line of sodden tents which flapped on the trampled mud, just beyond the midden, and at the glimpses of other tents arrayed about the meadows behind the screening trees. Perhaps he was thinking that this was the Belgium land for which he had come to fight. Perhaps he was remembering that these were the Flemish Netherlands where so often the English had pitched their tents and perished, and that the years would pass, and a death in 1918 didn't matter very much. The rain of a whole day had ceased, and the clouds, breaking, had let the sun through. The birds were spangling the evening with their bright notes.

He stood watching and listening. He wore no belt; but Tony, who stood behind him staring at his back, wore his Sam Browne across his breast like an officer on duty. One would have supposed that after a battle which had wrecked them, so that they were but flotsam on the high-water sand, they would have let the past go down with the wreck; but no, the Demiurge of War is not a man that he should pity, and his craftsmanship goes on: one wore a belt and the other did not.

'Kit,' said Tony.

There was no answer.

'Kit.'

Scrase heard, but seemed hardly interested: without turning round he mumbled, 'Er?'

'You've got to be ready to go down the line with me in about an hour,' explained Tony. 'After the battalion's moved off.'

Then Scrase turned round. His face was deathly pale and thin, as if thought had exhausted him as much as any disease; and the same exhaustion had emptied his wrists, which were attenuated and blue-white. He assumed, however, a laughing manner.

'Court-Martial, I suppose?'

Tony muttered a low affirmative.

'Well – ' Scrase shrugged his shoulders – 'that's the end of me, I suppose.'

Tony, his intellect beaten to dullness, could only answer feebly: 'Why fear the worst?'

'What can prevent it?'

'The M.O.s might put up a case for you.'

'Ah, but there's nothing wrong with me, Tono,' laughed Scrase – 'nothing that doctors can find. They can't see a man's will, and explain what happens when it suddenly ceases to work.'

'They might put up some sort of – er – mental plea.'

'But confound it, Tono, I've never been so clear-brained in my life. I seem to be seeing everything in the whitest possible light.' He sat down on the edge of the table and crossed his legs. 'And one thing I see very clearly, and it is that there's no explaining my case to a court of simple-minded old regular officers.'

'But, Scrase, old man – ' Tony walked up and down before continuing – 'try and explain it to me. If they'll let me I want to act as your Prisoner's Friend.'

'It's useless, Tono. You can't explain the gradual doubting of every decent principle under the sun and the loss of all purpose that results from it, and – my God! – the horrid acceleration of the heart, in those awful moments when your brain shows you with merciless clearness what such despair means. Can you explain *this*: that when I stood in that shell-hole before our attack, I told myself I would go over the top all right – and why not? I wasn't afraid – I cared too little – pooh! I wouldn't have minded if I'd been shot in the first seconds – but – but when the moment to advance came, my body didn't move. It simply didn't obey my will; it was as still as a clock when the spring's gone. The men went over, and five minutes later I was still there, and I sat in the mud and cried with disappointment. Can you explain that?'

Tony turned away his face, too miserable to answer.

'I can only plead "guilty"; and, Tono, isn't it funny, I'm not the least afraid of the firing party. I can think of it as vividly as I like and I don't turn a hair.'

'Oh don't!' pleaded Tony. 'Don't talk as if it were certain.'

'Of course it's certain. And I don't mind. At least, I don't mind going out. All that worries me is the thought of my people knowing the truth, and the men knowing. Gosh! it'll hurt the Alderman my father! If you knew him, you'd see why. He's a Tory of the Tories, and a typical City Father – ' Scrase smiled at the picture – 'I need say no more. By the way, do the men know?'

'They know you're under arrest, I suppose, but I don't suppose that they need know the – the issue.'

'But these sentences are published in General Routine Orders, aren't they?'

'I suppose so,' Tony agreed, and fumbled for his cigarette-case to gain time; 'but – ' he let the cigarette-case stay where it was – 'but don't you think that, with the battalion moving off like this into a new sector, and a new army, the – the story may never reach them?'

'I *don't*, Tono: I'm not such a fool. It'll be too rich a story. . . .'

'Nonsense, old man. They may never even know whether you were court-martialled or not.'

'What about the men whose testimony'll be taken?'

'I – well – but no one's been warned yet.' It was a poor answer, and Tony's heart registered its poorness by a sickly slowing. How could he compete in argument with Scrase, whose brain was moving as perfectly as his own was lumbering, if not stopping altogether? 'And . . . and, Kit . . . there are not many of the men left who knew anything about you, are there?'

'No. One can almost be glad of it.'

'Then again, if the rumour's true, we're going miles north, into the Nieuport sector.'

'Yes – Nieuport – and it's quiet there,' said Scrase, his eyes wandering with his thoughts away. 'You'll all have leave. . . .'

Tony gave no answer. His brain, defeated by simpler things, could not deal with this.

'Don't you think, Bungay,' asked Scrase smiling, 'that after they've passed sentence of death on a man, they should grant him a Last Leave?'

'Oh don't! . . .' It might have been Tony who was the sufferer, and Scrase the comforter. 'The worst hasn't happened yet.'

Scrase grasped his knee and whistled a few bars quite merrily. 'No, but it's inevitable.' He whistled a few more, while preparing his next words: 'Bungay, I've something to ask you. If the opportunity were to occur for me to – well, if by accident you were to leave your revolver on the table – would you explain to the Colonel that I didn't do it out of funk, but out of consideration for the regiment? He's a romantic old devil at heart, and he'd understand.'

'You mustn't talk like that,' murmured Tony.

'Seems a damn sensible way to talk,' answered Scrase, lifting his eyebrows humorously. 'It would stave off the disgrace to the regiment of a published conviction; it might even, as you suggest, be kept from the ears of the men so that they would never know what happened to me; and it would undoubtedly go quite a long way towards rehabilitating my name with the few who would know, for this funny old army is really as romantic as it can be, from top to bottom, as you've often pointed out, old Tono. No, it seems to me a great idea. And then . . . they would let it go through as "Killed in Action", which I confess would be a great relief to me. I know they would. I remember just such a case on Gallipoli. . . . Will you promise, then?'

'I promise nothing. You mustn't talk like this.'

'Doesn't really matter if you promise or not, old man, because if it happened, you couldn't help telling the Colonel of this conversation. And he'd understand. I can even imagine its rather appealing to him, if you told him that I said it wasn't cowardice which made me do it but – well – atonement, if you like.' He smiled at his words.

'We're talking nonsense,' Tony protested. 'I'm certainly not going to leave my revolver about.'

'I might run,' suggested Scrase, with eyes still smiling, 'and then you'd have to shoot. . . . But I don't want to do that. I don't want to be shot running, or by another hand.'

'Oh, shut up, old man,' Tony begged.

From the passage outside came Joe Wylie bringing two mugs of tea.

'There was some tea goin' downstairs, sir, and I thought you gen'l'men might like a cup. The men 'ave 'ad theirs, and are being fell in, and the Colonel and the Adjutant's gawn to march 'em off. It's quite lonely dahn there.' His next words were for Scrase. 'And 'ow are you feelin' nah, sir? Several of the men arst after you, and kindly, sir.'

'What did you say to them?' Scrase inquired.

'I said you was proper ill, that's all. I said, "I expect 'e's for 'awspital." ' By now Joe had placed a mug of tea on the table by the side of Scrase and given the other to Tony, who had walked away with it towards the window. Joe did not seem anxious to go, but stood with one hand twisting a button on his jacket. 'Well, now, sir – by the by, sir – did I ever tell you this one? Did I ever tell you 'ow – '

'Don't tell us now, Wylie,' Scrase interrupted, laughing again. 'Tell us later.'

'Here's the Colonel coming,' Tony warned.

'O my Gawd!' exclaimed Joe in a deliberately comical panic. And he fell to a panicky tidying of the room. A little comedy, a little jollity, was all the ministration he could offer to the pain in the room; and he wanted to offer something. 'The Colonel – Gawd help us! 'E's comin' up 'ere, you bet. . . . 'Ere, 'ow much time 'ave we got, sir?'

Scrase's thoughts seemed to return from straying. 'Er – what did you say, Tono?'

'The Colonel's coming across the fields. He's coming here, I think.'

'Oh, I – I'd rather not see him, unless I must. . . . I'll – I'll go in the other room and – yes, I can be packing.'

Forgetful of Wylie he went out hurriedly, crossed the passage and closed his door.

Joe heard the door shut and turned towards his officer. 'Don't it proper do you up, sir, to see him like that?'

'Yes,' agreed Tony.

'I suppose he realizes he's *for* it all right. Gaw! what on earth must he be thinking? . . . Does it seem quite fair to you, sir?'

'In what way?'

'It don't to me, sir. Ahter all, what's 'e done? Bitten awf a bit more of the poker than he could chew, that's all, sir. With a head-piece like his, he ought to 'a' bin a Staff Officer; then he'd 'ave 'ad a nice cushy job. But he chose to be with the Infantry – the boys that are getting on with the war – and he's stuck it aht long after he was a doner, and gaw lummy, sir! if you arst me, a feller that takes on a tough job and messes it up in the end may be as good a feller as 'im that takes on a soft job and gits through with it.'

'Surely, Wylie,' agreed Tony.

'Yes, and I mean: I admire 'im for it, because you never caught me takin' on the 'ard job if there was a soft one going. Nah, not on your life!'

'But you joined the Infantry, Joe,' Tony represented, 'when you might have joined the A.S.C. or something?'

'Yes, but jest to be along of some of me pals. And ain't I bin a-cussin' of meself for it ever since? And ain't I dodged the front line whenever it was possible? Gawd, yes! *you* know that, sir! Not 'alf!'

'You've done your bit, Joe, I think.'

'Not as '*e* 'as, sir. No, it's a shyme, I reckon. He done 'is best for the country, and now 'is country's goin' to start bullying 'im abaht and God-knows-what-all, instead of jest takin' 'im aht of the job which he's no good for any more, and usin' 'im in one which 'e'd do well. Strikes me the country's a chump, sometimes. . . . Is the Colonel comin' nearer, sir?'

'Yes, he's just at the door.'

'*Is* 'e? Well, good-bye, sir.' It was a comedian's exit such as Joe Wylie loved.

The Colonel's feet were on the stairs, and Tony waited for him. He entered in full marching kit, his revolver and map-case at his belt.

'Good evening, O'Grogan. I thought I'd better speak to Scrase before we move off.'

'Yes, sir.'

'How is he?'

'He's – he's resigned to the worst, sir. . . . Do you think he has a chance?'

'Not a ghost,' said the Colonel. 'This Passchendaele business has gone on too long. When you've got a Divisional Order posting policemen behind the attack to shoot any loiterers, dammit, they're not going to – they *can't* spare an officer.'

Tony bowed his head.

The Colonel's next words, so far as they could struggle through his inarticulateness, sounded apologetic. 'I had no course but to – Against my better judgement, I tried to know nothing about that hand of his – but when I discovered this other business I could not allow my private feelings – '

'He doesn't seem worried about himself, sir,' said Tony, coming to the Colonel's relief, 'but only about the disgrace to the regiment if he's shot, and the fear of his people getting to hear of it. He practically asked me to leave my revolver lying about.'

'*Ur?*' inquired the Colonel sharply. 'No, you can't do that. You can't do that.'

'He argued it out perfectly quietly, sir – almost jovially – that if he – er – did this, and if you understood that it wasn't cowardice, he would save the regiment the disgrace of it all, and perhaps rehabilitate himself – and – and perhaps you'd let it go through as "Killed in Action".'

'Poor fellow!' sighed the Colonel; and, bemuddled by the conflict in him now between the two forces of his mind – between the soldierly sternness which was his dream and the human kindness which was himself – he sat down and fell into a long silence. At last he said: 'No, it's too late to think of all these things now. . . . He should have . . . No, we can't monkey about like that. . . .'

'I suppose not,' Tony agreed; and as he said it, he was surprised by the sinking of his heart.

That sinking gave him sight: it brought right home to him the inevitability of Scrase's sentence; then the full realization of what such a calamity meant; then his own passionate resistance against it and his cold desire that anything other than this should happen to Scrase – *anything* – even the alternative which Kit himself had suggested. Oh yes, yes: a thousand times better that Scrase should have his way than that the Law should have its way with Scrase. The Colonel was seated and silent; and Tony was silent too as he paced up and down. Probably the Colonel's mind was stationary in its bewilderment: not so Tony's: behind a wrinkled and aching forehead, he was working up to the most difficult decision of his life. It was he who first spoke; and when he spoke he was surprised at the fluency which passion was giving him.

'Sir,' he began, 'I can't help thinking that, though legally there may not be the faintest chance for Scrase, we ought to be able to get round the Law somehow. We're English, and not Germans or French, ruthlessly scientific and logical and all that. I always like to think that the English have too much humour and horse-sense to sacrifice their souls to Law and to Logic – I mean: we often manage, if a man's technically guilty but morally innocent, to let a little good sense flood the situation and save him. There was a case on Gallipoli which delighted me at the time, when it was arranged behind the scenes that all the papers dealing with the technically guilty man should be "destroyed by gun-fire". I remember you laughed at the time and agreed that it was characteristically English.'

'I remember,' the Colonel acknowledged: "Corporal Player of the 19th East Lancs; yes, it was neatly done, that.' To his romantic mind such praise of his country was a sure appeal.

'Yes, and there was the case of Padre Quickshaw's D.S.O. the other day. That was the same thing, only inverted, wasn't it? The padre was technically guilty but morally praiseworthy, so instead of being stupidly logical about it, we walked round the Law and got him a D.S.O.'

'Quite,' agreed the Colonel.

'Well, then, sir – about Scrase. Of course, technically, he's as guilty as ever man was, but look at what he's done: three years' absolutely top-hole work in the regiment, when, as I believe, he was feeling perfectly putrid all the time. Oh, we can't – we can't be going to be so unhumorous as to shoot him. Surely – surely something can be done.'

The Colonel gave a long time to getting his disorganized brain around his subaltern's argument. Once or twice he started an answer and abandoned it, returning into himself. Tony stayed by the window, looking out. It must have been several minutes before the Colonel spoke.

'I'm afraid, O'Grogan, that things are different now from what they were in the first years of the war. Three years of it have knocked a good deal of our humour out of us, especially in high places.'

'I've noticed it,' said Tony. 'But it survives in the lower ranks. I think it'll always be there.'

'Yes. . . . Perhaps . . .' mused the Colonel. 'I'm impressed by what you say, O'Grogan. . . . I am really. . . . And I wish to God I could do something to save Scrase. . . . But it would be unfair to suggest that I thought there was any hope for him. I *know* there isn't. . . . On paper it's too black a case. First an S.I. and then – '

Tony wheeled round from the window.

'Then, dammit, sir, let us – let *us* have the humour to give him the chance he's asked for. Look here, sir: I'm in charge of him, and God knows what my penalty'll be for neglecting my duty, but I'm prepared to face that, and I'll – I'll go out and leave my revolver behind on the table. I'll' – the tears were in his voice now – *'I count* him just about my best friend, but I'm ready to be his executioner, if it'll save him any misery – if it'll mean that his men never hear that he was shot for cowardice, and his parents are told that he was "killed in action". I will, sir. I will, really.'

'No, O'Grogan. No,' stuttered the Colonel, 'dammit, you mustn't do that . . . I can't allow that. . . .'

With a sigh Tony turned back to his window. The charged silence possessed the room again.

'If anybody had to take the responsibility for a thing like that,' said the Colonel, '*I* would. Damn, O'Grogan! If it's hell for you, what's it for me who had to put him under arrest? . . .'

Silence again. Who could know what the Colonel was thinking? Some minutes later he also sighed, and looked at his wrist-watch.

'O'Grogan,' he ordered, 'go and tell Major Chamberlain that if I'm not there at the time, he's to march the battalion off himself. I shall follow.'

'Yes, sir,' said Tony woodenly – almost sullenly – and walked with studied smartness towards the door.

'And, O'Grogan: don't hurry back. I will be responsible here, and I may want to talk to Scrase.'

'Very good, sir. . . . Sir' – the sullenness was gone – 'you'll do what you can for him, won't you, sir?'

'Of course, O'Grogan.'

Tony went, and the Colonel sat alone – pondering – pondering. At one time his hand strayed down towards the revolver at his belt; but his expression and his falling hand showed that he had relinquished an idea which had visited him. Another time he turned his head towards the door as if to call Scrase, but relinquished this plan also.

It was Joe Wylie who put an end to his thoughts by coming into the room and saying:

'Gaw! I beg your pardon, sir. I thought you was Mr. O'Grogan. *My* mistake, sir.'

'You're Mr. O'Grogan's batman, aren't you?' asked the Colonel.

'Yessir.'

'I hope you're a little less slovenly than you were.'

'Yessir.'

'I've had my eye on you before, haven't I?'

'Well, yes, you 'ave, sir.'

'Er – ' A new idea seemed to visit the Colonel. He said to himself, 'H'm . . .' and then to Joe: 'You're the Regimental Humorist, aren't you?'

'*Wurl*, I shouldn't like to say that, sir.'

'But you have a talent for entertaining the men with stories, eh?'

'I do sometimes, sir.'

'And I suppose you think you've got the story of your life now.'

'How, sir?'

'With one of your officers under close arrest, and – whatever may happen to him.'

Joe brushed the knuckle of his forefinger under both sides of his moustache.

'It don't strike me as a funny story, sir. Rather the other way.'

'But it's a damned fine story to tell,' reminded the Colonel, fixing his eye on Joe. 'I suppose it would be asking a miracle to ask you not to tell it.'

'Not to tell what, sir?'

'Well, whatever may be the end of it all.'

'I wouldn't if you arst me not to, sir, and if it'd be any satisfaction to Captain Scrase.'

'What would you do when the men pumped you for information?'

'I'd tell 'em a power of lies if I 'ad to, sir.'

'Good!' said the Colonel, laughing, but with no real mirth. 'You can invent stories, eh?'

'I do sometimes make 'em up, sir.'

'Well, Wylie, what about never telling the true story but inventing a better one instead, eh?'

Joe was now staring back at the Colonel.

'I dessay I could think out something, sir.'

'Do it, then. You say you're sorry for him.'

'Yes, sir. If I may say so, *yes*, sir.'

'Right. Then you won't want to add more punishment to any he may have to take?'

At this Joe's expression clouded with a mild perplexity. '*Add* to it, sir?'

'Add the extra shame and disgrace which would come if it were talked about and known. His parents, you see.'

'Oh, I *know* them, sir. His father's Alderman Scrase in our Burrer – a fine old gen'l'man – '

'All the more reason why you shouldn't talk now or when you go on leave. It seems a small thing to ask you to give up this damned fine story, but I know enough of human nature to see that it isn't. . . . You will, though?'

'*Yurse*, sir. *You* trust *me*, sir.'

'All right. . . . H'm. . . .' The Colonel looked towards the door of Joe's room. 'Do you sleep in there?'

'Yessir.'

'H'm. . . . Well. . . . I suppose you're expecting to go on leave soon?'

'Yes, sir. I bin sweatin' on my leave for some time now.'

'I'll do what I can to put it through at once.'

'Thenk you, sir.'

Joe was moving towards the room when the Colonel, his eyes on the ground, called to him again. 'If you like to go and see the battalion off, Wylie, you may. You can tell Mr. O'Grogan I sent you.'

'I think I ought to be packin', sir. We're supposed to be moving off after the battalion – '

'Oh, damn that!' snapped the Colonel, irritably. 'That's all right. There's no hurry.'

'Right, sir. Then I think I will jest nip awf. Thenk you, sir.'

And Joe Wylie followed Tony out into the falling dusk. Colonel Tappiter sat on in his chair, rather dumpily, as if the battle in his mind was weighing him down. A misery of indecision, such as his, relaxed a figure usually erect. He heard very far away the voices of his officers shouting the orders of the march to the battalion, and the tramping of many feet as the battalion passed along the road by the farm-yard gate. The men, marching at ease, were whistling in unison, 'When we've wound up the Watch on the Rhine . . .' and they carried the tune away with them down the road. He stood up and went to the window, and saw the afterglow of the sunset behind the furthest trees. Then he looked towards the door of Joe Wylie's room. As if merely curious at first, he walked to the door and pushed it open. There was Joe Wylie's kit, neatly folded and piled on the floor, and his rifle leaning against the corner. He went in and picked up the webbing equipment, and looked at the ammunition pouches with their clips of cartridges. He dropped the equipment so that it fell back untidily on the folded blankets and ground-sheet. He looked at the rifle: it was clean, and he restored it to its corner. He came out and pulled the door after him, but not so that it latched; and he began the sentry-go of a frustrated thinker up and down the room. Up and down, up and down – oh God, for a decision! He took his debate back to the chair and sat down, wrestling with it still. His arm, lying along the table, kept automatically lifting up its hand and letting it fall; and later he discovered that he was examining his nails, and idly tending them. Well, one couldn't sit here for ever – O'Grogan would be back soon. 'Leave it to chance? I dunno.' Scrase: a good fellow; one of the best, really; had served him splendidly for three years all over the world. And now a firing party – a wall. Oh damn, no! The boy was right in asking an opportunity to escape from that. And young O'Grogan was right in all he said too. The boy could be given his opening, if – if he himself could make up his mind about it. For himself it would mean what? Understanding from the Higher Powers, probably, if he told the truth to the Court of Enquiry; or a mere censure, and there an end, did he plead guilty to no more than negligence in the matter: and in any case, the applause or the punishment that might be his – these were unimportant considerations. To stiffen his decision that the action itself was right, this was all that exercised him now.

But the action – oh, it was awful – he couldn't do it. . . . But if he didn't do it he left Scrase to his fate, and that was more awful. Was he to be a coward too, and just run away from an ordeal, and leave a boy to his fate? A firing party for Scrase? Damn! it *wasn't* thinkable. He rose up again and walked to the door of Wylie's room, and stood opposite for a while longer, before his will worked. Then with his foot he kicked at the door so that it swung open, disclosing the rifle leaning against the corner and the tumbled belt of cartridges lying on the kit.

Coming away and standing by the table once more, he called, 'Scrase'; and, not receiving an answer, called again.

'Sir!'

Scrase was leaving the room across the passage, and now came into his presence.

'I – er – thought I must say good-bye to you, Scrase. The battalion has gone, and I'm just going to follow it. I – er – wanted to say good-bye to you.'

'Thank you, sir. . . . Good-bye.' Nervously Scrase put out his hand, but the Colonel did not at once take it.

'And I should like to tell you that I am immensely grateful for all you've done, and – er – whatever happens over this wretched business, you can be certain that I shall – I shall do my best to insure that your parents hear only a good report of you. O'Grogan was telling me all you'd been saying about them.'

'Thank you, sir.' Scrase said it with a smile. 'I *was* a bit anxious about them.'

'Well, you needn't be. . . . No, I don't think you need be. . . . It's quite possible for me to pull all sorts of strings, you know. . . .' (When had he said those words before – *when* was it?)

'Yes, sir. And I – I should like to say that the only other thing that worries me is the thought of having brought disgrace on the battalion.'

'Oh, well . . . perhaps that won't happen. . . . You know that among the officers, at any rate, you are getting nothing but sympathy and – yes, I think I may say, admiration for your work in the past – '

'But there's no chance for me, sir, is there?'

The Colonel, suddenly afraid that his last words might have raised impossible hopes, looked him faithfully in the eyes.

'I'm afraid not, Scrase. . . . Forgive me, but I don't want to be dishonest with you.'

'No, sir. . . . I understand. Thank you.'

Colonel Tappiter stretched out his hand.

'Good-bye, then, Scrase.'

'Good-bye, sir,' said Scrase, taking the Colonel's hand firmly, who gripped his and held it. . . . 'But excuse me, sir, where's O'Grogan?'

'I – I sent him out for a bit, but he should be back soon. And his batman too – so you'll be alone for a little while.'

A curious look appeared on Scrase's face.

'Thank you, sir.'

'Oh, that's nothing . . . that's nothing . . .' and he released Scrase's hand. 'Well, I must be going. . . . Yes . . .'

And without another word he went quietly down the stairs. He passed out into the yard before the farmhouse and walked towards the gate in the roadside wall. There he turned and hurried back; but stopped and paused – and turned round again. Reaching the road, he walked a little way till the side of the house hid him from the view of the window of Scrase's room. There he waited. He saw O'Grogan returning, and moved as if to stop him – but paused again. If things were not to be as he had imagined them, they were *not* to be. In two minutes' time O'Grogan would be back in that room; and he himself could hurry off to his horse and his groom, and canter after the battalion. But even as he thought this, a shot rang out from a room in the farmhouse; and the Colonel, with a sharp intake of breath and a face very white, hurried back to it.

From: *The Jesting Army.*

ERNEST RAYMOND was born in Argentières, France, in 1888 and was educated at St Paul's School and Durham University. He is the author of, among other books, *Tell England* and *The Jesting Army.* He served on the Western Front (Ypres), at Gallipoli, and in Mesopotamia as a chaplain attached to the infantry.

THE PRAYER OF THE MEN OF DALESWOOD

Lord Dunsany

He said: 'There were only twenty houses in Daleswood. A place you would scarcely have heard of. A village up top of the hills.

'When the war came there was no more than thirty men there between sixteen and forty-five. They all went.

'They all kept together: same battalion, same platoon. They was like that in Daleswood. Used to call the hop-pickers foreigners, the ones that come from London. They used to go past Daleswood, some of them, every year, on their way down to the hop-fields. Foreigners they used to call them. Kept very much to themselves did the Daleswood people. Big woods all round them.

'Very lucky they was, the Daleswood men. They'd lost no more than five killed and a good sprinkling of wounded. But all the wounded was back again with the platoon. This was up to March, when the big offensive started.

A group of Morris dancers from Nothill, Bedfordshire.—From A COUNTRY CAMERA *by Gordon Winter.*

'It came very sudden. No bombardment to speak of. Just a burst of Tok Emmas going off all together and lifting the front trench clean out of it; then a barrage behind, and the Boche pouring over in thousands. "Our luck is holding good," the Daleswood men said, for their trench wasn't getting it at all. But the platoon on their right got it. And it sounded bad, too, a long way beyond that. No one could be quite sure. But the platoon on their right was getting it: that was sure enough.

'And then the Boche got through them altogether. A message came to say so. "How are things on the right?" they said to the runner. "Bad," said the runner; and he went back, though Lord knows what he went back to. The Boche was through right enough.

' "We'll have to make a defensive flank," said the platoon commander. He was a Daleswood man, too. Came from the big farm. He slipped down a communication trench with a few men, mostly bombers. And they reckoned they wouldn't see any of them any more, for the Boche was on the right, thick as starlings.

'The bullets were snapping over thick to keep them down while the Boche went on on the right: machine-guns, of course. The barrage was screaming well over and dropping far back, and their wire was still all right just in front of them when they put up a head to look. They was the left platoon of the battalion. One doesn't bother, somehow, so much about another battalion as one's own. One's own gets sort of homely. And there they were wondering how their own officer was getting on, and the few fellows with him, on his defensive flank. The bombs were going off thick. All the Daleswood men were firing half-right. It sounded from the noise as if it couldn't last long, as if it would soon be decisive, and the battle be won, or lost, just there on the right, and perhaps the war ended. They didn't notice the left. Nothing to speak of.

'Then a runner came from the left. "Hullo!" they said. "How are things over there?"

' "The Boche is through," he said. "Where's the officer?"

' "Through!" they said. It didn't seem possible. However did he do that? they thought. And the runner went on to the right to look for the officer.

'And then the barrage shifted farther back. The shells still screamed over them, but the bursts were farther away. That is always a relief. Probably they felt it. But it was bad, for all that. Very bad. It meant the Boche was well past them. They realized it after a while.

'They and their bit of wire were somehow just between two waves of attack. Like a bit of stone on the beach with the sea coming in. A platoon was nothing to the Boche; nothing much perhaps just then to anybody. But it was the whole of Daleswood for one long generation.

'The youngest full-grown man they had left behind was fifty, and someone had heard that he had died since the war. There was no one else in Daleswood but women and children, and boys up to seventeen.

'The bombing had stopped on their right, everything was quieter, and the barrage farther away. When they began to realize what that meant, they began to talk of Daleswood. And then they thought that when all of them were gone there would be nobody who would remember Daleswood just as it used to be. For places alter a little, woods grow, and changes come: trees get cut down, old people die; new houses are built now and then in place of a yew-tree, or any old thing, that used to be there before; and one way or another the old things go; and all the time you have people thinking that the old times were best, and the old ways when they were young. And the Daleswood men were beginning to say: "Who would there be to remember it just as it was?"

'There was no gas, the wind being wrong for it, so they were able to talk – that is, if they shouted, for the bullets alone made as much noise as breaking up an old shed, crisper like, more like new timber breaking; and the shells, of course, was howling all the time, that is the barrage that was bursting far back. The trench still stank of them.

'They said that one of them must go over and put his hands up, or run away if he could, whichever he liked, and when the war was over he would go to some writing fellow, one of those what makes a living by it, and tell him all about Daleswood, just as it used to be, and he would write it out proper, and there it would be for always. They all agreed to that. And then they talked a bit, as well as they could above that awful screeching, to try and decide who it should be. The eldest, they said, would know Daleswood best. But he said, and they came to agree with him, that it would be a sort of waste to save the life of a man what had had his good time, and they ought to send the youngest, and they would tell him all they knew of Daleswood before his time, and everything would be written down just the same, and the old time remembered.

'They had the idea, somehow, that the women thought more of their own man and their children and the washing and what-not, and that the deep woods and the great hills beyond, and the ploughing and the harvest and snaring rabbits in winter, and the sports in the village in summer, and the hundred things that pass the time of one generation in an old old place like Daleswood, meant less to them than the men. Anyhow, they did not quite seem to trust them with the past. The youngest of them was only just eighteen. That was Dick. They told him to get out and put his hands up, and be quick getting across, as soon as they had told him one or two things about the old time in Daleswood that a youngster like him wouldn't know.

'Well, Dick said he wasn't going, and was making trouble about it; so they told Fred to go. Back, they told him, was best, and come up behind the Boche with his hands up; they would be less likely to shoot when it was back towards their own support.

'Fred wouldn't go, and so on with the rest. Well, they didn't waste time quarrelling, time being scarce, and they said: What was to be done?

'There was chalk where they were, low down in the trench, a little brown clay on the top of it. There was a great block of it loose near a shelter. They said they would carve with their knives on the big boulder of chalk all that they knew about Daleswood. They would write where it was and just what it was like, and they would write something of all those little things that pass with a generation. They reckoned on having the time for it. It would take a direct hit with something large, what they call big stuff, to do any harm to that boulder. They had no confidence in paper, it got so messed up when you were hit; besides, the Boche had been using thermite. Burns, that does.

'They'd one or two men that were handy at carving chalk; used to do the regimental crest and pictures of Hindenburg, and all that. They decided they'd do it in reliefs.

'They started smoothing the chalk. They had nothing more to do but just to think what to write. It was a great big boulder with plenty of room on it. The Boche seemed not to know that they hadn't killed the Daleswood men, just as the sea mightn't know that one stone stayed dry at the coming in of the tide. A gap between two divisions, probably.

'Harry wanted to tell of the woods more than anything. He was afraid they might cut them down because of the war, and no one would know of the larks they had had there as boys. Wonderful old woods they were, with a lot of Spanish chestnut growing low, and tall old oaks over it. Harry wanted them to write down what the foxgloves were like in the wood at the end of summer, standing there in the evening, "Great solemn rows," he said, "all odd in the dusk. All odd in the evening, going there after work, and makes you think of fairies." There was lots of things about those woods, he said, that ought to be put down if people were to remember Daleswood as it used to be when they knew it. What were the good old days without those woods? he said.

'But another wanted to tell of the time when they cut the hay with scythes, working all those long days at the end of June; there would be no more of that, he said, with machines come in and all.

'There was room to tell of all that, and the woods too, said the others, so long as they put it short like.

'And another wanted to tell of the valleys beyond the wood, far afield, where the men went working; the women would remember the hay. The great valleys he'd tell of. It was they that made Daleswood. The valleys beyond the wood, and the twilight on them in summer. Slopes covered with mint and thyme, all solemn at evening. A hare on them perhaps, sitting as though they were his, then lolloping slowly away. It didn't seem, from the way he told of those old valleys, that he thought they could ever be to other folk what they were to the Daleswood men in the days he remembered. He spoke of them as though there were something in them, besides the mint and the thyme and the twilight and hares, that would not stay after these men were gone, though he did not say what it was. Scarcely hinted it, even.

'And still the Boche did nothing to the Daleswood men. The bullets had ceased altogether. That made it much quieter. The shells still snarled over, bursting far, far away.

'And Bob said tell of Daleswood itself, the old village, with queer chimneys, of red brick, in the wood. There weren't houses like that nowadays. They'd be building new ones and spoiling it, likely, after the war. And that was all he had to say.

'And nobody was for not putting down anything anyone said. It was all to go in on the chalk, as much as would go in the time. For they all sort of understood that the Daleswood of what they called the good old time was just the memories that those few men had of the days they had spent there together. And that was the Daleswood they loved, and wanted folks to remember. They were all agreed as to that. And then they said how was they to write it down. And when it came to writing there was so much to be said, not spread over a lot of paper I don't mean, but going down so deep like, that it seemed to them how their own talk wouldn't be good enough to say it. And they knew no other, and didn't know what to do. I reckon they'd been reading magazines, and thought that writing had to be like that muck. Anyway they didn't know what to do. I reckon their talk would be good enough for Daleswood when they loved Daleswood like that. But they didn't, and they were puzzled.

'The Boche was miles away behind them now, and his barrage with him. Still in front he did nothing.

'They talked it all over and over did the Daleswood men. They tried everything. But somehow or other they couldn't get near what they wanted to say about old summer evenings. Time wore on. The boulder was smooth and ready, and that whole generation of Daleswood men could find no words to say what was in their hearts about

Daleswood. There wasn't time to waste. And the only thing they thought of in the end was: "Please, God, remember Daleswood just like it used to be." And Bill and Harry carved that on the chalk between them.

'What happened to the Daleswood men? Why, nothing. There come one of them counter-attacks, a regular bastard for Jerry. The French made it, and did the Boche in proper. I got the story from a man with a hell of a great big hammer, long afterwards, when that trench was well behind our line. He was smashing up a huge great chunk of chalk because he said they all felt it was so damn silly.'

From: *Tales of War.*

LORD DUNSANY (Edward John Moreton Drax Plunkett, 18th Baron) the Irish story writer and dramatist, was born in 1888, educated at Eton and Sandhurst, and fought in the Boer War in the Guards and in the First World War in the Royal Inniskilling Fusiliers on the Western Front, where, in April 1916, he was wounded. He was Byron Professor of English Literature in Athens when the Nazis invaded Greece in the Second World War and was held by them but returned mysteriously to Dublin in 1942. Dunsany, who was the author of more than seventy books and plays, died in 1957, and was succeeded by his only son.

THE NIGHT PATROL

Taffrail

The night was intensely dark, with every indication of rain in the low, heavy-looking clouds and the damp, chilly feeling in the air. The young moon had long since set, but no stars twinkled overhead, for from horizon to horizon the arch of the heavens was shrouded in an impenetrable canopy of velvety, smoky black, with here and there the inkier blackness of bunches and wisps of scattered nimbus trailing lazily to the north-eastward on the wings of some freakish upper air-current.

On the surface it was quite calm, what little breeze there had been during the day having died away at sundown. And now, soon after midnight, the oiliness of the sea was only ruffled in little patches by occasional errant cat's-paws, as gentle breaths of air came stealing fitfully seaward from the direction of the coast.

To the east and the south-east, where lay the land, the under-

Cheering sailors on board HMS Vindictive *immediately after their successful Zeebruge raid on 23 April 1918.*—CAMERA PRESS LTD.

sides of the clouds on the horizon flickered and glowed spasmodically with a dull ruby light reflected from the gleam of distant and invisible gun-flashes. In the same direction, white balls of fire from star-shell and flares soared ceaselessly skywards, now in twos and threes, sometimes in sudden batches of a dozen. They curved over and down, shedding areas of bluish-white light, misty, but very brilliant, until, waning gradually, they fell slowly to earth, to be followed by others. And though those flares were fired ashore in the trenches many miles away, their illumination would have permitted those in the destroyer patrol watching off the coast to read moderate-sized print without difficulty. The trenches themselves must have been bathed in a glare as bright as daylight.

From somewhere on land, far away behind those leaping balls of fire, the narrow, misty beam of a searchlight, terminating abruptly where it met the clouds, wandered uneasily across the low sky. Another, nearer at hand on the coast, wakened into being at intervals, and sent its ray sweeping slowly to and fro across the sea, searching for it knew not what, like a great watching eye.

The still air throbbed in the insistent murmur of heavy gun-fire, now loud like thunder as the offshore breeze freshened, now hushed to a sound like the far-away rolling of many drums, or the soft rumble of a distant goods-train passing through a culvert. It was the song of the Western Front, the ceaseless song which had continued for nearly four years.

To those in the destroyers it was no novelty. No great offensive was in progress. Affairs ashore were in their normal condition, each side holding its own trench-lines, and contenting itself with nightly raids and uninterrupted bombardments of the opposing trenches and back areas. Those whose duty lay afloat had long since become accustomed to the sounds of strife, regarding them, indeed, as being quite in the order of things. Sometimes, when the firing seemed to quicken in its fury, they rather pitied the men fighting in the trenches, wondering vaguely how 'them pore blokes' were getting on, and secretly rather envious at not being able to lend them more of a helping hand in the common cause. But when the wind rose, and the short, curling sea made life a misery and a burden; when, in the bitter winter gales, the driving spray froze as it fell and glued men's mufflers to their necks, covered the always slippery decks with sheet-ice until it was barely possible to stand upright when the ship rolled, and choked the muzzles of the guns with blocks of solid ice, which had to be thawed out with hot water – then it was that the men at sea were jealous of those who fought on land, and had nothing whatsoever to do with that most unstable and unsympathetic element, the sea.

The work of the patrolling destroyers was certainly no sinecure. They had occasional spells off, but sometimes for a fortnight or more they were at it night after night in all weathers, taking what rest they could in the day-time. There had been many 'scraps' with German torpedo-craft – short, sharp, desperate encounters in the blackness of the night, when the combatants, rushing practically alongside each other at high speed, pumped shell at their opposite numbers at point-blank range, and dodged and twisted madly in their efforts to ram and to use their torpedoes. They were always breathless, rather nerve-racking experiences, these battles in the darkness. They began so suddenly, and when one least expected them. Events succeeded each other with nightmare rapidity, while the element of chance entered hugely into them. One might make up one's mind what to do in fifty different combinations of circumstances, but it was always the fifty-first that happened. The Germans, moreover, though it is true they generally sought safety in flight when once engaged, were desperate fighters when it came to the point, and frequently gave as many hard knocks as they got.

The enemy always had the advantage in that they could emerge from their ports at their own chosen time. There was no knowing when or where they might appear, and the watchers, spread out in groups over a large area, had always to be ready. When, as it sometimes happened, month after month passed without incident, the work of the patrols, always arduous, seemed rather purposeless and monotonous. The inactivity – to call it that for want of a better word, for they were always busy – might have lulled some people into a sense of false security, encouraged them to relax their efforts, to take things a little more easily.

But not so these men. There was hardly a destroyer working in the area which, at one time or another, had not been blooded in actual close-quarter conflict with the Boche. Every officer and man knew his work. Each one of them realized that the ship which sighted the enemy before the enemy sighted her, and was thus enabled to get in the first salvo of shell, or the first torpedo, generally had the opponent at her mercy. Even if the foe appeared in superior strength it mattered little. Again and again it had been proved by actual experience that these night destroyer actions normally ended in close-range *mêlées*, in which, before very long, the ships of both sides became hopelessly mixed. So superiority in numbers was usually countered by surprise. In other words, the side which struck first, and struck hard, generally won.

Moreover, and what was far more important, these outlying destroyers were the advanced sentries for a complicated system of other patrols behind them, not to mention an army of other craft – auxiliary patrol-vessels engaged in their usual task of hunting and harrying submarines, transports and hospital-ships passing to and fro across the Channel, merchantmen – ships of every possible persuasion and calling.

There had been regrettable incidents in the past, when German destroyers, favoured by mist and low visibility, had slipped through the cordon of watchers to bombard towns, to sink and destroy ships, and had succeeded in making their escape without being brought to action. Such things did not happen through any defect in organization, or through any lack of zeal or energy on the part of the patrols. They were merely the outcome of bad luck, the ever-changing fortune of war.

Nevertheless, when such incidents took place, certain sections of the public press raised their voices and clamoured mercilessly for somebody's blood, inquiring, in terms both impolite and acid, what the navy was thinking about to permit such goings-on.

They little knew the conditions in which the patrols worked, did not realize a tithe of their responsibility, or that, to any seaman, it was manifestly impossible for every square mile of sea in the Strait to be watched and guarded constantly. They forgot that the hostile raids, regrettable though they might be, were only part and parcel of the ebb and flow of war. It is impossible to make omelets without breaking eggs, impossible to make war without loss; while, after all, the sallies which the Germans occasionally indulged in with varying success were only comparable to those nightly raids in the trenches.

No; some people ashore who had the satisfaction of sleeping in their beds every night of their lives forgot that there had been no appreciable tightening of their belts, and quite omitted to remember to what and to whom this was due.

And the navy, when attacked by the Scribes and the Pharisees, its own countrymen, those whom it fed and defended, merely shrugged its shoulders and said nothing. It had been pilloried in the past, and would doubtless be pilloried in the future. It knew the fickleness of public opinion; recollected, with some little bitterness, that at one port men wounded at the battle of Jutland had been hissed and execrated while being carried ashore on their blood-stained stretchers.

Such things should not be, but unhappily are; so the Sea Service, being wise in its generation and too proud to explain, smiled, said nothing, and – continued to do its duty without the plaudits of the multitude.

The watchers continued to watch.

II

On board the *Minx*, the third destroyer in the line, M'Call, the first lieutenant, was keeping the first two hours of the middle watch. He stood close to the bridge-screens, using his glasses continually to sweep the horizon, with an ever-watchful eye upon the black smudge and the dim trail of phosphorescent water which showed the position of the ship next ahead, a cable distant. Occasionally, as the ship crept up or dropped astern of her station, or sheered a little out of the line, he flung an order over his shoulder to the man at the revolution telegraph, or to the helmsman twiddling his wheel as he peered into the dimly lit compass-bowl, the men repeating the orders word for word, to show they had been heard and understood.

Besides M'Call himself, the quartermaster, and the man at the engine-room telegraphs, space had also to be found on the small bridge for a couple of A.B.s, who had nothing to do but keep a constant look-out to port and to starboard, a leading signalman, the messenger, and two more men, whose duty was to attend to the instruments and the voice-pipes communicating with the guns and the torpedo-tubes. There was hardly room to move, no space whatsoever to walk up and down.

At the first lieutenant's feet, coiled up in an impossible attitude in a deck-chair tucked in under the chart-table, lay Langlands, the lieutenant-commander, seemingly asleep. He and his second in command invariably spent the entire night on the bridge when the ship was on patrol, relieving each other every couple of hours for the doubtful comfort of the deck-chair. It was a miserable sleeping-billet at the best of times, and bitterly cold; while as often as not one or both of the officers spent the hours of darkness without a wink of actual sleep. But neither would dare trust himself off the bridge for a moment when there was the least possibility of the enemy being sighted. It was their station in action.

The sub., lucky fellow, spent his watch below, slumbering more or less peacefully on the settee in the charthouse, a concession he generally made up for by keeping extra watch in the day-time. As for the gunner and the midshipman, R.N.V.R., the latter a young gentleman who was still at a public school in 1916, they, fully dressed, were sleeping, or pretending to sleep, in some hole or corner near the stations they would occupy in action, the 'snotty' somewhere in the forepart of the ship, near the foremost 4-inch gun, and the gunner by his beloved torpedo-tubes. The engineer-lieutenant and the surgeon-probationer were the only officers who could turn in in their clothes with really clear consciences, though the former had elected to make himself a bivouac on deck with blankets, a rug, and an air-pillow within six feet of the hatch leading to his engine-room. He was a wise man, was the engineer officer, and a married man with a large family. He had once been in the wardroom of a destroyer when a mine exploded under the stern, and since that distressing experience he preferred being on deck. The surgeon-probationer either did not know of, or did not care for, such things. He lay stretched out on a settee in the stuffy wardroom, snoring blissfully.

Men, some dozing, but the majority wide awake, lay clustered round the guns, the torpedo-tubes, or the searchlight, prepared for an instant summons. Shell and cartridges were piled in all the gun-positions, where the loading numbers could find them easily in the dark; while at various places on deck were bundles of cutlasses, and rifles with magazines charged and scabbarded bayonets fixed, ready for immediate use in the event of running alongside an enemy and boarding. All the officers and some of the men carried automatic pistols or revolvers in belts strapped round their thick lammy coats; while two unshaven gentlemen, one an ex-grocer's assistant from Bermondsey, and the other a Glasgow newspaper-boy, presided drowsily over a couple of machine-guns.

In a word, the ship was prepared for action. A single touch on the bell-push on the bridge by the first lieutenant's elbow would set the alarm-gongs jangling and bring the men jumping to their feet.

The night, except for that constant rumble of gun-fire in the east, was very still. There was no whistling of wind through the rigging, nothing but the hiss, gurgle, and liquid splutter of the bow-wave as the ship moved through the water, the deep humming of the stoke-hold fans, and the occasional shrill, protesting cry of a startled and indignant diver disturbed in his beauty-sleep on the water and scuttering clumsily for safety.

The sub., in the charthouse, awakened by the conversation of the gun's crew sitting on deck outside, was softly anathematizing them.

'I met 'er at the cinema last time I was on long leaf,' said a voice. 'Fine, strappin' gal she was. Reg'lar little bit of all right. She takes a fancy to me the minute – '

'Go hon, you ruddy old Bluebeard!' came a gruff interjection. 'What about that other gurl I used to see you walkin' out with?'

'Can't 'elp the other gal,' was the rather indignant reply. 'She played me false. I found out she was bein' courted by a lance-corpril belongin' to a bantam reg'ment. I 'ad a dust-up with 'im about it; but she weren't worth fightin' over, so I just said 'e could bloomin' well 'ave 'er. This one I'm tellin' you about takes a fancy to me the moment she claps eyes on me.'

'She can't know much about you, Shiner.'

'What d'you mean? Can't know much about me!' with some acerbity. 'What d'you mean, speakin' like that? Why should she want to know about me? She loves me at first sight, I tells you!'

'Go hon, you old liar!' was the polite retort.

'S'welp me, she did! She takes me 'ome to see 'er pa and ma, and they likes me, too, 'cos they asks me to stay and 'ave a bit o' supper. 'Er pa works in Pompey dockyard. 'E and 'is missus likes their drop o' gargle now and then, so the nex' night I does the polite and treats 'em all to seats at the 'Ippodrome, and a bit o' somethin' t'eat at a restorong afterwards. Cost me more'n 'arf-a-quid, that did. And now it's all fixed up proper, and me and Lucy gets married nex' time I goes on long leaf. Fine, strappin' bit o' fluff, she is. Got a bit o' money in the bank, too!'

'Can't you fellers let a bloke get a drop o' sleep, 'stead o' chawin' your fat all the bloomin' night?' growled a new and very irritated voice. ' 'Oo wants to hear about your love conquests, Shiner?'

'I'll 'ave you know I'm engaged to the young lady,' came the dignified answer. 'Any bloke what says a word agin' 'er gets a punch on the nose! See?'

'Well, you might let other blokes get a bit o' sleep, anyhow.'

'Oh, go to 'ell!' said Shiner wrathfully. 'You don't know what bein' in love feels like. 'Oo's goin' to fall in love with a bloke with a face like yourn?'

'Ssh!' hissed someone. 'Don't get having a barging-match, you two. You'll wake Little Jimmy in a minute. He's asleep in the chart-house.'

'Oh, go to 'ell!' retorted the amorous one.

The sub-lieutenant, rather pleased that his newly discovered lower-deck nickname was not 'Dirty Dick' or 'Sweaty Sam', chuckled softly to himself, examined his wrist-watch, discovered he had still over an hour before he was due on the bridge, and rolled over and went to sleep again.

III

Presently, as the destroyers reached the limit of their patrol, M'Call, on the bridge, saw the long, dark shadow of the leader swinging out of the line as she altered course to starboard to proceed in the opposite direction.

'Captain, sir,' he said, bending down to shake the recumbent figure in the deck-chair by the shoulder, 'they're altering course.'

'Right!' grunted the lieutenant-commander, sitting up and fumbling for his pipe. 'Follow 'em round. Are we up to time?'

'To the minute, sir. The tide's been against us during the last run.'

'Right! Let's see. High-water's at 1.42, our time, isn't it?'

'Yes, sir.'

'So, if we have to go skiboosting about over these blessed banks after the Huns, there'll be water enough for us up till about half three – what?'

'There or thereabouts, sir. We might say four o'clock at a pinch.'

'That be blowed for a yarn!' smiled the C.O. 'Not in these trousers! What about that fellow who smashed up his rudder and propellers the other day by leaving it a bit too late? The Court of Inquiry had his blood, all right; and I'll be shot if you'll persuade me to become a burnt-offering!'

'You mean the *Galeka*, sir?' laughed the first lieutenant, watching the next ahead as her helm went over. 'Of course! It's become a habit with her. Sheds propellers by the dozen, and is always in dock expectin' other people to do her dirty work. Damn stoopid, I call it. What sort of a ship goes messin' about on an eight-foot bank, and she drawin' ten and a bit? *We* don't do silly things like that, thank the Lord! Not often, anyhow. Port fifteen, quartermaster!'

The lieutenant-commander seemed rather amused.

'The *Galeka* made a mistake of an hour over this beastly B.S.T.

business,' he pointed out. 'I don't wonder at it, personally; but if I were you, Number One, I shouldn't say too much. She's not the only one who's slipped up, not by a very long chalk. What about the time you – '

'Port twenty!' M'Call interrupted, anxious to avoid a question which he had every reason to know would be awkward. 'Ease to ten!' as the ship swung round after her leader. ''Midships! Meet her starboard! Steady! What was it you were going to say, sir?' he inquired.

'I've forgotten now,' Langlands yawned. 'But let me know when we turn again, and if I find you astern of station you'll be hanged, drawn, and blooming well quartered.'

'I will bear it in mind, sir,' replied Number One, quite unperturbed.

It must have been about twenty minutes later that M'Call, who was intently watching the horizon through his glasses, grunted with surprise. Was his imagination at fault, or had he really seen something – something vaguely white and indistinct – far away in the darkness?

'Starboard look-out,' he asked, lowering his binoculars to wipe the object-glasses, 'did you see anything fine on the starboard bow just now?'

'Thought I saw a sort o' sudden splash,' the man answered. 'Thought maybe 'twas a fish jumpin', or a breakin' sea, sir.'

'Can't have been a sea,' said M'Call, rather puzzled; 'it's flat calm.'

'That's what it looked like to me, sir,' the seaman protested, rather annoyed at being doubted. 'There, sir!' after a pause; 'there it is again!' He pointed at a glimmer of white with a triumphant forefinger.

The officer's glasses flew to his eyes, and the briefest inspection satisfied him that the man was right, for there slowly crept into his field of vision a ghostly looking streak of whitened, splashing water. He did not linger an instant, but shouting, 'Action!' pressed the bell-push in front of him.

The time was twelve and a half minutes to two.

The alarm-gongs whirred and jangled throughout the ship, and even as their strident chatter died away he could hear the men bestirring themselves on deck, and the shuffling of feet as they closed up round their guns.

'Action stations!' roared a voice. 'Show a leg, boys! Look lively now!'

'What is it?' asked Langlands, already on his feet.

'Bow-waves on the starboard bow, sir!'

'All right,' the skipper answered, seemingly quite unmoved by the information, but feeling his heart fluttering with excitement. 'I'll take the ship. You look after the gunnery.'

'Ay, ay, sir. Hicks!'

'Sir?'

'Pass down: All guns load with lyddite; bearing – green,* three, five; range – one, four, double o; deflection – one, five, right.'

'That's them all right!' murmured the captain, with his glasses to his eyes, as the dim flicker of a flaming funnel broke out of the darkness. 'Damn bad stoking, too! Is the sub. up here?'

'Yes, sir.'

'Warn the tubes to be ready to starboard. Don't fire until you get orders.'

'Increasing speed, sir!' sang out a signalman, as the lumped-up water in the wake of the destroyer ahead grew whiter and more distinct. 'Leader altering course to starboard, sir!'

Langlands, his glasses still levelled on the approaching enemy, flung an order over his shoulder to the man at the telegraph, and the *Minx*, throbbing to the increased thrust of her turbines, darted forward.

The glimmering bow-waves were now clearly visible to the naked eye, and even as the commanding officer watched them, he saw first the whitened trails of water in the wake of several fast-moving vessels, and then the long, blurred smudges of the ships themselves,

* The side on which a target happens to be is always passed down as 'green' or 'red', to avoid possible confusion between the words 'starboard' and 'port'. The order 'Green – three, five', would mean that the guns were to be laid on an object on the starboard side, 35 degrees from right ahead. Similarly, 'Red – one, two, o', would signify that the target was to port, 120 degrees from right ahead.

dimly silhouetted against a lighter patch on the horizon. They were something over a mile distant.

'How many d'you make out, Number One?' he asked.

'Three or four, sir,' said M'Call, putting his lips to a voice-pipe to pass another order to the guns.

'They don't seem to have spotted us,' the captain went on. 'Perhaps they can't see us against the dark background to the west'ard. Are you all ready?'

'Yes, sir. Quite ready.'

The natural sound of his own voice comforted him, for Langlands, though certainly no coward, was not one of those abnormal men who could saunter through the very gates of hell without trepidation in their hearts. In such people heroism and calmness in the face of danger is a natural habit which can cost them little. They actually do not know what fear is, and hence have no difficulty in combating it.

Another species of bravery altogether is shown by those who feel fear, but can manage to stifle it – can make their will triumph over the perfectly natural desire for personal safety.

And Langlands had this quality. He had been in action many times; but always, before the firing began, his sensations were the same – a ghastly dread of the unexpected, a sickly feeling of apprehension, and an apparent loss of control of his body and limbs, as if his muscles were suddenly made of jelly. But his mind was ever active in such conditions. His brain worked fast and clearly, and outwardly his demeanour was just the same as usual. The fear he felt in his innermost heart never made itself manifest. He had trained himself to conceal it, and even went so far as to smoke a pipe in action to convince others that he was in no way perturbed. Artificiality perhaps, but his men noticed it, and took courage.

It was the suspense that was so intolerable, the awful period of waiting between the time the enemy were sighted and the firing of the first shot. It might be seconds or it might be minutes; but it always seemed hours – hours of mental anguish and nerve-racking anxiety. Once under fire, however, these sensations left him altogether, and all thoughts of his own personal safety, all terror of the unknown, were brushed aside. He became cool and alert. Then followed the period of wild exultation when his chief desire was ever the same – to get to close quarters; to fight, if need be, with his bare fists. Realization, he found, was never quite so bad as anticipation. It was the thinking beforehand of what might happen that was so maddeningly unnerving.

The orders for the destroyers on patrol were very simple and elastic, and all the commanding officers knew exactly what was expected of them. They knew the exact speed at which the leader intended to fight, and that, until they came into close action, they had only to conform to his movements. Complications really began when the engagement became general and the formation was broken, for then it was a case of each ship for herself, her duty to single out an opponent, and, if possible, to stick to him until he was crippled or sunk.

They were at liberty to use their own initiative, taking what chances they were offered of ramming or of using their torpedoes, and utilizing their gun-fire to the best possible advantage. Beyond that, nothing else much mattered; and if, in the *mêlée* which was almost bound to ensue, any friendly vessel had the ill-fortune to be stopped or sunk, it was an understood thing that her crew would have to take their chance until the close of the engagement. Their mates could not break off the action to succour them. The orders were very definite on one point – that while a British ship could steam and a British gun could fire, the raiders were to be pursued, hotly engaged, and reported.

By this time the enemy was at a distance of little more than a thousand yards, and, still steaming fast on a roughly parallel and opposite course, seemed quite oblivious of the presence of the British. It was scarcely possible that he had not sighted them, for even with the naked eye Langlands could clearly see the humped-up, unfamiliar shapes of the German destroyers, with their two squat funnels standing nearly upright, the tall masts aft, and the shorter ones forward. There was no mistaking them.

Perhaps they took the British for friends. Maybe they were merely reserving their fire, or were trusting to their speed to slip past without giving battle, for not a light twinkled down their line, not a gun roared out. They still steamed steadily on, grim, menacing, and silent. There were five of them.

The flotillas must have been drawing together at a combined speed of fifty knots, possibly more, and if both continued their courses they would flash by each other at a distance of about four hundred yards. And at fifty knots, one thousand yards is covered in thirty-six seconds; but still the British leader held steadily on his course. The seconds dragged – the enemy came nearer and nearer – the suspense became maddening. Langlands felt his heart thumping like a sledge-hammer. Was the leader missing his opportunity? It seemed as if in another few seconds it would be too late!

But the senior officer was an old hand at the business, and knew what he was about, and at exactly the right moment his helm went over, and Langlands saw the leading destroyer swerving abruptly to starboard until she was heading straight for the centre of the hostile line. It was evidently the senior officer's intention to attempt to ram the fourth or fifth ship, leaving those ahead to the other destroyers under his orders. It was the plan agreed upon, the plan they all knew by heart.

There came a blaze of greenish-golden flame and the crash of a ragged salvo as the leader's guns opened the ball. A little cluster of spray fountains, white and shimmering, leapt out of the dark sea close to the leading German, and almost before they had tumbled out of sight the guns were flashing all down the hostile line. In another instant every British ship replied and the firing became general.

The time was 1.49.20.

The guns were firing at point-blank range, so that careful aiming, even if it had been possible, was unnecessary. The din became deafening as the loading numbers crammed projectiles and cartridges home, the breeches of the guns slammed to, and the gun-layers pressed their triggers and fired. The air thudded and shook. Intermingled with the deep roaring of the heavier weapons came the unmistakable stutter of the two-pounder pom-poms as they fell to work to sweep the opposing bridges and decks, and the shriller stammering of Lewis guns and Maxims. Projectiles screeched and whinnied overhead, burst with a dull, crashing explosion, and sent their fragments humming and hissing through the air to strike funnels, hull, and deck fittings with an insistent jangling clatter like pebbles in a tin can. Machine-gun bullets sprayed past in droves, swishing and crackling as they came like raindrops through foliage.

Langlands, all but blinded by the brilliant flares of the *Minx*'s guns, held steadily on his course. The water round the ship seemed to be spouting and boiling with falling shell, and all he could see of the enemy was the flashes of their guns bursting out redly through a leaping curtain of shell-geysers, and clouds of dense, rolling smoke. The Germans seemed to be altering course a little, for the ship the *Minx* was making for, the third in the line, was drawing slightly across the bows.

'Port ten!' he ordered breathlessly, intent on running her down.

'Port ten it is, sir,' came the deep voice of the coxswain, as he twirled the wheel.

''Midships! Steady so, Baker!'

'Steady it is, sir!'

A searchlight from some ship in the German line flickered into brilliance, illuminated the scene for an instant in its sickly glare, and then was suddenly extinguished.

There came a crash, an explosion, and a momentary blaze of reddish fire from amidships, as a shell drove home by the *Minx*'s after-funnel; but Langlands paid little heed, for the ship still sped on. Another projectile detonated on the water close under the bow, and a signalman on the bridge sat down with a grunt of stupefied astonishment, and began cursing softly to himself. The coxswain, with his right arm broken by a piece of the same shell, groaned audibly as he tried to use the limb and felt the jagged ends of the bone grating horribly together. He suffered excruciating torment, for, unknown to himself, another sliver of red-hot steel had penetrated the muscles of his back. He was in agony, but he still watched the captain, waiting for his next order, and casting an occasional glance at the compass before him to keep the ship on her course.

A red Very light, soaring aloft, bathed the scene in a momentary flush of crimson before, curving over, it fell hissing into the water. The crashing, thudding medley still went on, but above the din M'Call could be heard passing orders like an automaton, and without a tremor in his voice. He passed his orders, but he little knew that the man below whose duty it was to transmit them to the guns was stretched out on deck, slowly sobbing his life away.

'Can I fire, sir?' suddenly screamed the sub., hoarse with excitement.

'Yes!' the captain shouted back, without turning his head.

And a moment later, when the boy saw the flame-spouting silhouette of the enemy's leader in line with the sights of his instrument, he pressed an ebonite knob, shouted through a voice-pipe, and looked anxiously aft. He was rewarded, for he saw the dull bluish flash and the silvery streak of a torpedo as it leapt from its tube and plunged with a splash into the water. Where that particular torpedo went he never knew, for there was no resultant explosion.

But an instant or two later, when the second German came in line, he pressed another knob. The range at the time seemed absurdly short, and the enemy flashed by in an instant, but the weapon went home. It seemed to strike her fairly amidships, for there came a lurid blast of flame and a cloud of greyish smoke and spray, followed by the roar of an explosion which for a moment completely drowned the sound of the guns.

'Got her, by George!' the sub. muttered softly to himself, watching her as the turmoil subsided and he caught a glimpse of the dripping bow and stern of the enemy's ship lifting themselves out of the water, with the middle portion sagging horribly. 'Clean in halves!'

He had never seen the effect of a torpedo before, and could hardly believe his eyes.

Then several things seemed to happen all at once.

A torpedo fired by the enemy, travelling on the surface in a flutter of spray, suddenly shot past within ten feet of the *Minx*'s bows, and almost at the same moment the destroyer astern of the one which had been torpedoed crashed into her helpless consort with a grinding, splintering thud which could almost be felt. The firing from both ships ceased abruptly, and a chorus of shouts and screams came out of the darkness.

The collision occurred within about two hundred feet of the *Minx*'s bows, so close and on such a bearing that Langlands could hardly avoid the tangle.

'Hard a-starboard!' he yelled, however, unwilling to risk damaging his own vessel by running down an enemy which must already be helpless through having been collided with by a friend. 'Hard a-starboard, Baker!'

The coxswain flung the wheel over with all his strength, but it was too late.

The ship slewed, but a moment later Langlands caught a hasty glimpse of the black hull of his enemy right under the bows. He found himself looking down on her deck; could see the blurred, white faces of her men as they stared up at him; heard their frightened screams as they saw this new monster bearing down upon them to complete their destruction. It must have been a terrifying sight, the towering, V-shaped bow tearing remorselessly towards them at over twenty knots, with the twin bow-waves leaping and playing on each side of the sharp stem.

A gun roared off from somewhere close at hand, and with the orange flash of it Langlands felt his cap whirled off his head and something strike him across the forehead. A warm gush streamed down his face; but in the excitement of the moment he scarcely noticed it.

The next instant the ship struck.

There was a rending, shuddering thud, the shrill, protesting sound of riven steel, and then a sudden cessation of speed. The hostile destroyer, struck in the stern, twisted round with the force of the blow, and heeled bodily over until the water poured over the farther edge of her deck. Then the *Minx*'s bows tore their way aft, splintering, grinding, and crunching – enlarging the enormous wound, wrenching off the side plating, and allowing the water to pour in. The stern of the enemy slid free, and it could be heard slithering along the starboard side as the *Minx* still drove ahead.

The time was exactly 1.52. Four and a half minutes since the enemy had been sighted; two and a half since the first gun had been fired. It had seemed an eternity.

Out of the corner of his eye Langlands caught sight of the shape of one of his friends, spouting flame, driving past to starboard and circling madly across the *Minx*'s bows; while another shadow, vague and indistinct in a smoke-cloud, and with guns silent, flashed past, travelling to the north-eastward at high speed. It was the German leader escaping.

For a while the flashes of guns still broke out of the darkness from the direction in which the scattered remnant of the enemy, pursued and hotly engaged, were flying for their lives. The flashes gleamed golden and ruby, while an occasional shell-burst showed up as a flicker of smoky scarlet. The flashes receded farther and farther towards the horizon, and the sobbing, pulsating thunder waned gradually, fainter and fainter, as the combatants streamed away. Then the rolling thud of a distant heavy explosion, and save for the dull mutter of the guns ashore the night was still.

About an hour later, when the pursuers returned, they found nothing but an area of sea strewn with the wreckage of sunken ships, the unmistakable flotsam of battle. They lingered on the spot to rescue several badly wounded and half-drowned Germans who cried piteously for help; but of the *Minx* there was no trace.

'*Minx!* Oh, *Minx!*' they asked by wireless. '*Minx*, where are you?'

But the *Minx* did not answer, and it was with a touch of sadness in their triumphant hearts that the victors picked their way back over the rippling sandbanks towards the anchorage in the golden-grey light of the dawn.

IV

The rain-clouds had cleared away, but with the advent of daylight a dense sea-fog lay close and thick upon the water; and through it three battle-scarred destroyers steamed wearily but proudly home towards a certain English port whither they had been ordered for necessary repairs.

All three exhibited plain traces of the fight. One, with an enormous gash on the water-line in the engine-room, caused by a bursting shell which had put the port turbine out of action, limped painfully along at a bare ten knots, with her pumps working to keep down the flow of water, and a collision-mat plastered over the orifice. Another, the leader, had her bridge wrecked, her foremost 4-inch gun useless, and a number of jagged holes through the forecastle; while the grey hulls, upper works, and funnels of all three were torn and perforated by shell-splinters, and mottled here and there by the unmistakable yellow splashes and charred paint where projectiles had struck and detonated. They looked as if they had undergone a severe gruelling, as indeed they had; but their casualties were remarkably light – no more than seven killed and thirteen wounded.

It was nearly noon when, with new White Ensigns fluttering gaily from their mizzens, they steamed jauntily into harbour through the entrance between the well-known grey stone breakwaters, each crowned with its white lighthouse.

The fog had cleared a little. The time of their arrival had been reported by wireless, and as they entered a bunch of signal-flags went up to the truck of the admiral's flagstaff ashore. An instant later the men-of-war at their moorings seemed suddenly to swarm with men.

'Oh lor!' grunted the senior officer of the incoming destroyers, realizing what was about to happen as he conned his ship from the battered bridge. 'Hell and scissors! I always feel such a damned idiot on these occasions! Never know what to do.'

And a few moments afterwards, as the leader passed within a hundred feet of a huge, blister-sided monitor, the signal ashore came down with a rush, and the monitor's men, waving their caps, broke into a roar of frenzied and uncontrolled cheering, which was taken up by ship after ship. It was no ordinary three cheers. It was a noise like the yelling of the crowd when a goal is scored at a popular football match, a deep-throated bellow which reverberated across the water and echoed and re-echoed from the cliffs. It was an encouraging sound, a sound of good-feeling and good-fellowship, very genuine and spontaneous; and nobody can make more din than the sailorman when he is happy and really puts his heart into it.

The sea-front was densely packed with civilian spectators, who had heard vague rumours of a naval engagement, and even they shouted themselves hoarse and waved parasols, hats, and handkerchiefs as the three destroyers slid up to their buoys.

'I'm glad they're pleased,' murmured the senior officer, blushing a rosy red and rubbing his unshaven chin. 'I do feel a sanguinary fool, though, and I wish to Heaven they'd stop their beastly row! I can't hear myself think.'

'Signal, sir,' said the yeoman of signals, who had been busy with his telescope. ' "Vice-admiral to division. Well done. Congratulate you most heartily on your success. Admiral would like to see commanding officers when convenient. *Minx* reports – " '

'Minx!' shouted the S.O. in delighted astonishment. 'Has she got back, then?'

'Seems so, sir,' said the yeoman, looking round with his telescope. 'Yes, sir,' after a pause. 'That's her! They're just putting her into the floating dock. Her bows are smashed up somethin' crool, and her topmast has gone over the side.'

'Ah, that accounts for our getting no answer to our wireless signals,' murmured the commander. 'Thank Heaven, she's in, though!'

He meant it.

'On the night of the 28th–29th four of our destroyers on patrol met five enemy craft on their way to take part in a raid in the Channel. A hot engagement ensued, in the course of which three of the enemy were sunk. The other two, hit repeatedly and hotly pursued to their base, succeeded in escaping in a badly damaged condition, though from aerial reconnaissance it is believed that one of them subsequently foundered. We lost no ships, and our casualties, considering the close range at which the action was fought, were very slight. All the next of kin have been informed.' – *Official Communiqué*.

'*TAFFRAIL*' (Captain H. T. Dorling, R.N.) was born in 1883 and educated at H.M.S. *Britannia*. He entered the Navy and served in the China War of 1900, the South African War, and throughout the First World War. He was the author of many books about the sea, the war, and adventure.

'The maintenance of the Dover Patrol is a story in itself. Occasionally the enemy tries to raid it.'—SIR ERIC GEDDES
11 July 1918.

MARCHING ON TANGA

Francis Brett Young

The spot which the brigade had reached the night before, where we now rejoined them, lay within earshot of a great stretch of rapids, in thin bush scattered with boulders. A pleasant camp, if it had not been for the intense heat which the moist air of the river seemed only to increase. Here we were well guarded, for the Baluchis and Punjabis had been thrown out some miles ahead. When we arrived the Gurkhas, of which the Kashmiri regiments are mostly composed, were busy catching the small blue barbel of the Pangani, and the whole camp wore an aspect of security and comfort. Reports from the front were hardly reassuring. The hills, which sloped to the right bank of the river in this part of its course, were stony and seared by many deep nullahs, which made it almost impossible to build roads for any but the lightest transport. For two days the 61st Pioneers had been hard at work cutting bush and banking the

German officers with Askaris near Tanga, in German East Africa. —BAYER HAUPTSTAATSARCHIV *Munich.*

track, but they had not advanced more than four miles in this difficult country, while beyond the region of stony nullahs stretched a wilderness of swamps, impassable in the rainy season, and still, for all we knew, beset with difficulty. More than this we did not know. All the river valley above our objective, M'kalamo, appeared to be clogged with thorn of an unusual density, so thick, indeed, that aerial reconnaissance was useless.

But somehow a move must be made if we were to keep pace with Hannyngton, now marching down the railway towards Mombo, and slowly dislodging the enemy whom it was our duty to intercept at his bridgehead. On the evening of the 8th my section was ordered to move forward from the riverside camp (Kitumbatu) to join a flying column under Colonel Dyke, composed of his own regiment, the 130th Baluchis, the 29th Punjabis, the 61st Pioneers, and the 27th Mountain Battery. With us we were to carry rations for two days, but no other kit: our heavy panniers were to be left behind as well as all wheeled transport. We must look forward, we were told, to a march of over twenty miles through appalling country and a scrap at the end of it. Everything depended on the speed of our movement....

That evening the light section, with T . . . and myself, marched on over the road which the Pioneers had already made as far as the Baluchis' camp, where Colonel Dyke lay sweating under an awning with a bundle of maps and airmen's sketches and reports. It was a pity that neither were very reliable. That night we made a cold meal of bully beef and biscuit. It was the last food I was to taste for forty hours.

We moved off at dawn, immediately in the rear of the Mountain Battery. No Indian Regiment can show a finer set of men. Sikhs, and picked Sikhs, led by the best gunner officers in India and equipped with all the care that goes to a crack corps. Now, as before, our way was shown us by the Pangani, beyond which, to our left, rose the mountain masses which the enemy were supposed to have evacuated the day before. In three places foot-bridges spanned the river, at every bridgehead a village, and these were so slender that we might look upon this flank as secure.

As the sun rose the day became very oppressive, with a clouded sky. Luckily, in this part, the going was easy and the bush sparse.

The battery mules, with their guns in sections on their backs, moved at a great rate. A tremendous pace had been set by the long-legged Baluchis in front, and in the first hour the whole column covered more than four miles : a fine achievement when you consider what one is apt to forget when thinking of all these operations : that the country was not only difficult but actually within a few miles of the Equator, at a latitude in which as a rule the white man rests under shelter from early morning till sunset. Indeed the pace began to tell a little on some of our men, old campaigners though they were. In ordinary times we should have given them a lift on our ambulances, but here we had no wheeled transport, and the poor devils had to shift for themselves.

By eight o'clock we had travelled nine miles, reaching an open space in which the rest of the brigade were to camp for the night. It lay opposite the mountain called Ngai and the village of Mheza, and we called it the Mheza plain, though it was really little more than an open sandy level. When we passed by, a string of natives came out from the village over the foot-bridge, and walked alongside us with easy strides. A very different type, these, from the painted Masai. In figure they were spare and dignified, with the fine carriage of the Arab : their features too were nobly modelled as those of the Arabs, which showed us, if we were in need of encouragement, that we had reached a zone where the coastal influence was felt in physical types if not in culture. All the men carried weapons : spears with polished shafts of wood and wide blades of an exceedingly graceful form. They walked beside us, I say, and spoke no word; they did not even talk amongst themselves, and, though they bore us company until we were at the level of the next village, did not seem to be very curious of our numbers or equipment. Then they vanished as mysteriously as they had come.

In the next hour we covered only three miles : the pace had been too hot to last. And now the character of the country began to change, as if indeed we had left the highlands. The trees, even the thorn bushes slung with nests of the bottle-bird, grew bigger : their leaves were more green. In addition to the everlasting acacia the baobab reappeared, rising from among tall grasses. The heat was suffocating. I watched T . . . riding ahead of me on the mule Simba. He leaned forward in the saddle as though he wanted to rest his head on something. He didn't tell me that he was ill, but I guessed from his languor and his flushed face that he was starting an attack of fever – an old enemy which he had reason to dread. . . . Thus we marched, painfully, for another two hours, at the end of which halts became more frequent. Evidently the position was not quite obvious in front. We were such a small column that the advance-guard moved only a few hundred yards in front of my bearers, and we were all prepared for action at any moment.

At length we emerged into the swampy zone which we had been expecting. An immense reed-bed separated us from the river, and beyond its belt of acacias rose the mountain named Mafi, beautifully wooded, and in particular a single peak with a white scar of bare cliff on its face, of a peculiarly lovely shape. For a long time I gazed at this white-scarred hill till I knew all its contours by heart. And, as it happened, it was well that I did so. The track, which was in places black and oozy as a road through a peat bog, kept closely in touch with the edge of the reed-bed. It was narrow, so narrow that all our column passed along it in single file; and this part of our progress, walking singly under the screen of the tall reeds, struck me as vaguely charged with expectation. Something must happen very soon, otherwise we could not be moving so very silently and so carefully hidden. The sense of something impending was so strong that I took special notice of the moment and of the scene. No one spoke; the feet of our mules made no sound in the soft earth; but one heard the gentle swish of grasses swept by the moving column. A pair of doves fluttered away from the path. A flight of weaver-birds swept the sky. We could hear the whirr of their wings. And then, without any warning, a shell screamed overhead, bursting fifty yards on our right. . . . This time we had not to deal with the 4-inch naval guns, but with the 80-millimetre quick-firer, which our men called the 'Pip-squeak', because the burst of the shell followed so quickly on the first report, and its scream was so shrill. Still we moved on secretly, and in absolute silence. The Germans must have been firing at a venture, for we were too well concealed for their observers to have seen us. At any rate, now we were in touch with them and matters might be expected to move swiftly.

But the swamp ended, and in its place we came upon dense bush, bush of a density such as we had never seen before. To deal with it the Pioneers were almost helpless. Even in single file we could not make our way. And the enemy knew that we were there. They must have guessed, for that matter, that we were thus entangled. In that thorny trap they might have raked us with their machine-guns, and in a short time Dyke's flying column would have been finished with. But nothing happened. Even the quick-firer ceased troubling us. The dense bush fell to absolute silence but for the lamentations of the hornbills, calling to one another in hollow tones. We moved forward in a series of strange gyrations. We stopped. To the torments of heat and thirst was added a sense of suffocation in the dead air of this close bush, too dense ever to have been swept by a clean wind, and charged with the aromatic odours of the bruised brushwood, a little like verbena but pungent, as the air of a greenhouse in summer with all its windows shut. We halted, waiting for a way to be found.

Our Kavirondo bearers sprawled upon the ground in attitudes of fatigue. Poor T . . . dismounted. He could hardly sit in the saddle for his fever was now at its height. He sat with his head in his hands. All of us, all of us were thirsting for air, clean air untainted by these vegetable odours and the stink of black flesh.

We moved on with a jerk . . . only for a few yards. It had not been worth getting up for that. And then we set off again for a hundred yards or so. I looked at my compass and found that we were heading due west, whereas the general direction of our march was south. We halted; turned again . . . this time south-east. Then due west again. We were wandering about in the bush as if we had been led by a hoodwinked man. In a little while, I thought, we shall find ourselves under their maxims. Probably we shall walk right into them. And then the fun will begin. Halting and struggling a few paces forward we spent another hour. Thank God there was no dust: so much, at any rate, we were spared. Several men were sent back to us who had been knocked out by the sun . . . sun and exhaustion, and want of food: it came to the same thing. And still there was no end, nor even the least infinitesimal thinning of the bush: just the eternal thorn of mimosa and acacia, set with brushwood and spearheads of wild sisal below, tangled with fleshy cactus above – scattered here and there with withered candelabra-trees lifting their dry arms above the thorn: over all the closeness of a heavy sky and the unutterable melancholy of the hornbill's hollow note.

But we had not very long to wait now. Somewhere in the thick bush in front of us Maxim fire crackled out. The Baluchis had bumped them. We halted, unloaded the panniers. Obviously this was no place for a dressing-station; but it was doubtful if anywhere in this unchanging bush we should find a better. T . . . was fit for nothing.

In front the firing increased in violence, its sounds magnified in an extraordinary degree by the echoing bush. Now our machine-guns, too, were in action. And then the wounded began to dribble in, Baluchis all of them; and our stretchers went out for the others who could not walk. Evidently, as usual, when our forces stumbled on a prepared position in the bush – and indeed the first evidence of its existence was generally a burst of Maxim fire – they had lost heavily in the first minute. There was no way out of it; these were losses which were inherent in the type of warfare and not to be avoided by any refinements of caution.

Soon I was busy stripping off the field dressings and seeing for myself that the wounds were rightly classified. My *babu*, fat and a trifle deaf, stood near, and hindered rather than helped. The bush seemed hotter than ever. I threw off my tunic and belt, haversack and water-bottle and worked in my shirt sleeves. Two Baluchi subalterns were brought in on the point of death with shattering head wounds. A bloody business: strong and fair young bodies both of them. The aromatic air smelt now of iodine and blood.

Indeed it was hot work single handed; for T . . . was as busy as his fever would let him be in getting a shallow trench ready for the seriously wounded, a pit scraped in the crumbling, fibrous ground just deep enough to give them the moral support of a sense of shelter. I worked maybe for an hour, maybe for two. I have said already that we made our dressing-station, as best we might, on the very edge of the track which the Baluchis had trampled in the bush; and now as I worked I had a fugitive vision of many men marching by, scarcely turning to look at me with my bloody arms, the patient figures of the wounded, the more patient shapes of the dead. They swung by unceasingly and their swift, unending progress carried with it a sense of gallantry and inexorable strength. I had not time to watch them or speak with those of them I knew; but very soon I saw the striped brown flashes of the Rhodesian helmets moving past. I could hardly believe it. They must have marched like the devil; for they had started five miles behind us. Nor did they march as tired men. The Maxims were rattling in front, and when one goes into battle one does not know fatigue. And thus, while we dressed our wounded, the whole brigade filed past. At any rate we were well protected. But the firing never slackened.

Another officer of the Baluchis was brought in with his thigh broken by a gunshot wound. He was in great pain, suffering, too, from shock of that surprise. The stretcher journey had shaken him, and he begged for morphia. He had already taken some; but I gave him another injection, for a wounded man will stand almost as much as you like to give him. About this time we found that we were short of water. That which had been jolted for twenty-four hours in our leaky *pakhals* had given out, so we sent four stretcher-bearers through the bush to the river with empty *chhagals* to be filled. In a little time they returned, very excited. There were askaris, German askaris, many of them, down by the river; on this side of the river, between us and the river. Several shots had been fired at them and they dared not go again.

It sounded like an excuse of the ingenuous kind which the African is fond of making; but all of them had the same tale, and all were genuinely scared. The thing sounded impossible. It implied a force working round the rear of the brigade of which they could not be aware. We sent a messenger straightway to the Brigade Headquarters. I do not know if he ever arrived there, but if he did it was too late.

Over the road on our left we heard scattered rifle fire. The wounded officer awoke from his morphia dose.

'My God,' he said, 'they're coming . . . they're coming.'

That is what bush fighting does for a man's nerves. . . . We assured him that it was nothing, that the whole brigade was between us and the enemy; but he could not be calmed. 'Get me out of this for God's sake,' he cried. 'If they find me like this . . .'

We all knew very well what would happen if the Germans' savages found him like that, and so we shifted the poor beggar a little deeper into the bush, near the place where the two subalterns lay still with blankets over their faces. And he seemed a little happier, sighing with a sort of content. I don't know why.

Again the rifle fire broke out on the left: very near this time. Another stretcher was brought in, and on it a man with a chest wound. I knelt down beside him, and started stripping the bloody bandage from his side. His skin was very cold. And then I suddenly saw that he was dead. I covered him with a blanket. The firing started again. It seemed very close now. A twig, snapped by a singing bullet, fell beside me on the dead man's blanket. Surely there must be something wrong . . . and then I saw some Kashmiris who were trudging along the road drop down suddenly in the dust and start firing into the bush. So the stretcher-bearers' story had been true, and now they were coming. In a second the whole place was swept with Maxim fire, hellishly loud in the bush, and bullets were singing everywhere. Luckily most of the fire was high. T . . . was busy trying to get the wounded officer deeper into the bush. Another murderous burst of fire. We all kept low. Indeed I was sheltering behind the body of the dead sepoy on the stretcher. The wounded men whom I had dressed and sent to lie down under a tree were getting restless. I counted seven of them, all, providentially, with wounds of the arms or body. And then, without any warning I saw the Gurkhas, who had lain firing in the roadway, scramble to their feet and come running towards me. One clutched me by the arm. '*Jaldi karo . . .* make haste, Sah'b,' he cried.

Our stretcher-bearers and ward orderlies were scattering in every direction. I shouted to the wounded Baluchi jemadar to keep the wounded men together. He didn't know English, but for all that he seemed to understand. Keeping as low as we might, we crawled out of the bullet-swept area and ran into the bush. Five Africans who had been lying under the thorns joined us. We were fifteen men in all with one rifle between us.

We halted, breathless. For a moment the firing had stopped. Then they came with a rush, sweeping through the dressing-station, now inhabited only by the dead, and then, having found it empty, hot upon our track. There is very little about bushcraft which the German askaris do not know, and the track made by fifteen men is easy enough to follow. A pause . . . and then a few scattered rifle shots: the whistle of bullets very near. They had found us. We could hear them crashing through the bush. The machine-gun started again.

There was nothing else for it. We must run. At any rate the density of the bush assured us of relative protection and might serve to handicap the movements of the German machine-gun. Besides, I thought, they would not dare to advance much further behind our lines. In a moment their heart would fail them and we should shake them off. We set off, scrambling through the bush as fast as we could go, and our pace was the pace of the slowest of the wounded, a ghastly Baluchi with a bullet through his chest. And then, to my horror, the bush suddenly ended. We came without warning to one of those wondrously beautiful glades of waving grasses with which the thorn is scattered. All down the Pangani we had seen them waving their purple heads in the sun; but here the country was more parched and the waves were silver. A lovely sight, and very easy going; but to cross it would have meant certain death. We might indeed have tracked forward towards the south and our own firing lines, but we did not know on how wide a front the Germans were advancing, and if we had moved for any distance at right angles to their course we should almost certainly have been killed or captured. Our only chance lay in keeping to the bush around the glade of grasses. If they had any idea of our strength the Germans would not hesitate to cross the open ground and cut us off. But obviously they hadn't. For one moment the jemadar, who was the last of us, saw a white man with a Maxim on the edge of the bush; then he disappeared and for a moment there was silence, until the askaris picked up the trail once more and began to search the bush with rifle fire.

My wounded men were lasting badly, and particularly the poor fellow with the wound in the chest. The bush was as dense as any I had seen in Africa, and almost entirely of thorn. There was only one way of penetrating it: to lower one's head, sheltered by the wide helmet, and dive through, heedless of torn clothes or flesh. As long as the eyes were safe, the rest of the body did not matter. But we were men unused to bushcraft or wounded, and whenever we paused for breath the askaris gained upon us and bullets droned through the wood, snapping the branches of the thorn-trees. It seemed as if we could never be free of them.

And I suppose they thought that here was a chance too good to be missed of taking prisoners, for they probably guessed we were a small picket party thoroughly scared. Our track in the bush would tell them, near enough, how many we were. If only that track could be concealed . . .

I ordered my party to scatter over a wider area, preserving as well as they might the main direction. For a little while they tried to obey me, but fear drove them together again; scared men are happier in a herd. The main direction in which I had tried to move was diagonally towards the north-west, in which quarter our divisional troops must soon be moving up; but every time that we pointed to the north, the enemy seemed to turn us west again with their fire. We were like birds being beaten from a cover. By now we knew that we were quite cut off from our own people, and approaching, perhaps, the line along which the Germans had planned their retreat.

And yet, harried though we were, I do not think that my mind was ever clearer in its view of the emergency, or, for that matter, more sensitive to the amazing beauty of the evening, the blue shadows on the mountains, the silvern beauty of that waving deadly grass. I desired passionately to live, though I hardly hoped to do so. And this was a strange discovery that came to me: that though a man who is running for a train or in a race can be utterly exhausted, a man who is running for his life cannot. So splendidly omnipotent was the will to live that the flagging muscles knew no fatigue. It was now twenty-four hours since we had tasted food, and yet I was not hungry. I had a feeling that the spirit of man is never so magnificently the master of his body as when he is facing death. And still we struggled on. The silver grasses became amber in the mellower evening light. That was our hope, our greatest hope of escape, the falling of darkness. Never was darkness so long in coming. I remembered a poem of the lover Meleager in which he prays for night. And I thought of my wife and of our home in Devon, a drowsy afternoon of summer in a garden ravished with the spicy odour of pinks. A strange business this . . . a strange business, that I, torn and bleeding, should be running for my life through the heart of Africa, through dense thorn which had never yet been shadowed by man's figure or penetrated by his violence since the beginning of the world: while, at home, perhaps, she whom I loved most dearly was sitting in that summer garden among so many peaceful scents and knowing nothing . . . knowing nothing. It seemed incredible that this could be at all. The sense of the natural limitations of a man's sensibility, the mere fact that for one of us, who were so near, to have realized the other's desperate case would have been labelled supernatural, overwhelmed me. One is told that the instinct of self-preservation drowns every other faculty in a desperate man. It doesn't. Each moment I expected to be shot or taken prisoner; but never, for one moment, did I lose grip on the imaginative significance of the scene, or of its beauty, or of the exaltation which told me that I might have been lying riddled with the many bullets which missed me in the dressing-station before the enemy rushed it.

And now, thanks be to God, the light was failing a little . . . for five minutes, perhaps, we had been unaware of our pursuers. We came, in the thick of the bush, upon a muddy creek, some tributary of the Pangani, with pools of slimy water clouded with mosquito larvae scattered up and down. Down on their knees fell all my company, scooping up the water in their curved hands. I did not drink. I was thinking of the next move, and of how, if the fight had ceased, I might get them back to our own people. And I, who had always carried a water-bottle, didn't quite realize the preciousness of that shocking water in the dry bush. We heard a few shots on our left. . . . So we hadn't quite done with them. I remember so well the sight of our little group standing very still and expectant, listening . . . just listening.

We clambered up the far side of the gully and pierced its screen of thorns. Now it really didn't matter how much we were torn. But what *did* worry me was that the wounded men were obviously failing in their strength. I was sorry, in a way, that we had stopped for water, because that respite of a few seconds from the terror of pursuit had given them time to remember their wounds and to think how exhausted they ought to be. We beat through a few yards of thorn and emerged upon yet another little creek, or else a new gyration of the last one. And here I saw our greatest chance of salvation. We were, indeed, in a great swamp. I told the rest of them to follow me exactly, and led them a strangely twisted course, crossing and recrossing the gullies, turning sharp in my tracks, making an utterly baffling maze of footprints. At the end of it I felt considerably safer.

Then suddenly, we heard them near, and stood quite still. This, it seemed, was the end. At the best we must be taken prisoner. I nearly made up my mind to take the risk of going out into the open. There was one white man there, with the Maxim. I might call out to him that we were a party of wounded and I a doctor; but my Red Cross brassard (if that were any good) had been left behind on my discarded coat, and I should probably be shot before I could prove my identity. One of my ward orderlies, indeed, was wearing a brassard. Supposing I borrowed this from him before I stepped out. . . . Perhaps there were only askaris there. A brassard would make no difference to them, and I should be killed, and the wretched ward orderly robbed of whatever safety the symbol might ever have given him. Or again; I might be saved and he might suffer. It wasn't good enough. . . . Very well, let them find us!

They didn't. Dead still we stood, hearing them come quite near. And then we heard them go away. I suppose night had fallen. In the swamp, at any rate, it was pitch dark; and from the innumerable slimy pools of the gullies arose a shrill chorus of frogs. This sound, so characteristic of the tropic night, made me realize suddenly the vast animation of the bush through which we had been fighting our way for our very lives, and its complete indifference to the end of our struggle . . . so small a piece of savagery in that cruel land. . . . It brought the whole incident down to its proper proportion. It would have been easy, I dare say, to indulge in heroics or thank Providence on one's knees. It didn't take me that way. I sat down on the thorns – what did I care for thorns? – with my heart going like a steam-hammer, and laughed out loud.

FRANCIS BRETT YOUNG was born in 1884, was educated at Epsom College, then took his medical degree at Birmingham University. He practised medicine at Brixham from 1907 until 1914, when he joined the Royal Army Medical Corps. After serving in East Africa he was invalided out with a sixty per cent disability from malaria in 1918. He and his wife went to live in Capri and he began trying to earn a living as a writer. He won the James Tait Black Memorial Prize in 1927 with *Portrait of Claire*, then subsequently wrote some twenty novels, in which, according to J. C. Squire, 'the poet, physician, romancer, and novelist collaborated'. He died in 1954.

THE LAST SOLO

Ian Hay

It was dawn on Saturday morning, and the second phase of the Battle of the Somme was more than twenty-four hours old. The programme had opened with a night attack, always the most difficult and uncertain of enterprises, especially for soldiers who were civilians less than two years ago. But no undertaking is too audacious for men in whose veins the wine of success is beginning to throb. And this undertaking, this hazardous gamble, had succeeded all along the line. During the past day and night more than three miles of the German second system of defences, from Bazentin le Petit to the edge of Delville Wood, had received their new tenants; and already long streams of not altogether reluctant Hun prisoners were being escorted to the rear by perspiring but cheerful gentlemen with fixed bayonets.

Meanwhile – in case such of the late occupants of the line as

A soldier crossing the street during the capture of Péronne by the Fifth Australian Division, on 3 September 1918.

were still at large should take a fancy to revisit their previous haunts, working parties of infantry, pioneers, and sappers were toiling at full pressure to reverse the parapets, run out barbed wire, and bestow machine-guns in such a manner as to produce a continuous lattice-work of fire along the front of the captured position.

All through the night the work had continued. As a result, positions were now tolerably secure, the intrepid 'Buzzers' had included the newly grafted territory in the nervous system of the British Expeditionary Force, and Battalion Headquarters and Supply Depots had moved up to their new positions.

To Colonel Kemp and his Adjutant, Cockerell, ensconced in a dug-out thirty feet deep, furnished with a real bed, electric-light fittings, and ornaments obviously made in Germany, entered Major Wagstaffe, encrusted with mud, but as imperturbable as ever. He saluted.

'Good morning, sir. You seem to have struck a cushie little home this time.'

'Yes. The Boche officer harbours no false modesty about acknowledging his desire for creature comforts. That is where he scores off people like you and me, who pretend we like sleeping in mud. Have you been round the advanced positions?'

'Yes. There is some pretty hard fighting going on in the village itself – the Boche still holds the north-west corner – and in the wood on the right. "A" Company are holding a line of broken-down cottages on our right front, but they can't make any further move until they get more bombs. The Boche is occupying various buildings opposite, but in no great strength at present. However, he seems to have plenty of machine-guns.'

'I have sent up more bombs,' said the Colonel. 'What about "B" Company?'

' "B" have reached their objective, and consolidated. "C" and "D" are lying close up, ready to go forward in support when required. I think "A" could do with a little assistance.'

'I don't want to send up "C" and "D",' replied the Colonel, until the Divisional Reserve arrives. The Brigade has just telephoned through that reinforcements are on the way. When they get here, we can afford to stuff in the whole battalion. Are "A" Company capable of handling the situation at present?'

'Yes, I think so. Little is directing his platoons from a convenient cellar. He was in touch with them all when I left. But it is possible that the Boche may make a rush when it grows a bit lighter. At present he is too demoralized to attempt anything beyond intermittent machine-gun fire.'

Colonel Kemp turned to Cockerell.

'Get Captain Little on the telephone,' he said, 'and tell him, if the enemy displays any disposition to counter-attack, to let me know at once.'

Then he turned to Wagstaffe, and asked the question which always lurks furtively on the tongue of a commanding officer.

'Many – casualties?'

' "A" Company have caught it rather badly crossing the open. "B" got off lightly. Glen is commanding them now: Waddell was killed leading his men in the rush to the final objective.'

Colonel Kemp sighed.

'Another good boy gone – veteran, rather. I must write to his wife. Fairly newly married, I fancy?'

'Four months,' said Wagstaffe briefly.

'What was his Christian name, do you know?'

'Walter, I think, sir,' said Cockerell.

Colonel Kemp, amid the stress of battle, found time to enter a note in his pocket-diary to that effect.

Meanwhile, up in the line, 'A' Company were holding on grimly to what are usually described as 'certain advanced elements' of the village.

Village fighting is a confused and untidy business, but it possesses certain redeeming features. The combatants are usually so inextricably mixed up that the artillery are compelled to refrain from participation. That comes later, when you have cleared the village of the enemy, and his guns are preparing the ground for the inevitable counter-attack.

So far 'A' Company had done nobly. From the moment when

they had lined up before Montauban in the gross darkness preceding yesterday's dawn, until the moment when Bobby Little led them in one victorious rush into the outskirts of the village, they had never encountered a set-back. By sunset they had penetrated some way farther; now creeping stealthily forward under the shelter of a broken wall to hurl bombs into the windows of an occupied cottage; now climbing precariously to some commanding position in order to open fire with a Lewis gun; now making a sudden dash across an open space. Such work offered peculiar opportunities to small and well-handled parties – opportunities of which Bobby's veterans availed themselves right readily. Angus M'Lachlan, for instance, accompanied by a small following of seasoned experts, had twice rounded up parties of the enemy in cellars, and had despatched the same back to Headquarters with his compliments and a promise of more. Mucklewame and four men had bombed their way along a communication trench leading to one of the side streets of the village – a likely avenue for a counter-attack – and having reached the end of the trench, had built up a sandbag barricade, and had held the same against the assaults of hostile bombers until a Vickers machine-gun had arrived in charge of an energetic subaltern of that youthful but thriving organization, the Suicide Club, or Machine-Gun Corps, and closed the street to further Teutonic traffic.

During the night there had been periods of quiescence, devoted to consolidation, and here and there to snatches of uneasy slumber. Angus M'Lachlan, fairly in his element, had trailed his enormous length in and out of the back-yards and brick-heaps of the village; visiting every point in his irregular line, testing defences; bestowing praise; and ensuring that every man had his share of food and rest. Unutterably grimy, but inexpressibly cheerful, he reported progress to Major Wagstaffe when that nocturnal rambler visited him in the small hours.

'Well, Angus, how goes it?' inquired Wagstaffe.

'We have won the match, sir,' replied Angus with simple seriousness. 'We are just playing the bye now!'

And with that he crawled away, with the unnecessary stealth of a small boy playing robbers, to encourage his dour paladins to further efforts.

'We shall probably be relieved this evening,' he explained to them, 'and we must make everything secure. It would never do to leave our new positions untenable by other troops. They might not be so reliable' – with a paternal smile – 'as you! Now, our right flank is not safe yet. We can improve the position very much if we can secure that *estaminet*, standing up like an island among those ruined houses on our right front. You see the sign, *Aux Bons Fermiers*, over the door. The trouble is that a German machine-gun is sweeping the intervening space – and we cannot see the gun! There it goes again. See the brick-dust fly! Keep down! They are firing mainly across our front, but a stray bullet may come this way.'

The platoon crouched low behind their improvised rampart of brick rubble, while machine-gun bullets swept low, with misleading *claquement*, along the space in front of them, from some hidden position on their right. Presently the firing stopped. Brother Boche was merely 'loosing off a belt', as a precautionary measure, at commendably regular intervals.

'I cannot locate that gun,' said Angus impatiently. 'Can you, Corporal M'Snape?'

'It is not in the Estamint itself, sirr,' replied M'Snape. ('Estamint' is as near as our rank and file ever get to *estaminet*.) 'It seems to be mounted some place higher up the street. I doubt they cannot see us themselves – only the ground in front of us.'

'If we could reach the *estaminet* itself,' said Angus thoughtfully, 'we could get a more extended view. Sergeant Mucklewame, select ten men, including three bombers, and follow me. I am going to find a jumping-off place. The Lewis gun too.'

Presently the little party were crouching round their officer, in a sheltered position on the right of the line – which for the moment appeared to be 'in the air'. Except for the intermittent streams of machine-gun fire, and an occasional shrapnel-burst overhead, all was quiet. The enemy's counter-attack was not yet ready.

'Now listen carefully,' said Angus, who had just finished scribbling a despatch. 'First of all, you, Bogle, take this message to the telephone, and get it sent to Company Headquarters. Now you others. We will wait till that machine-gun has fired another belt. Then, the moment it has finished, while they are getting out the next belt, I will dash across to the *estaminet* over there. M'Snape, you will come with me, but no one else – yet. If the *estaminet* seems capable of being held, I will signal to you, Sergeant Mucklewame, and you will send your party across, in driblets, not forgetting the Lewis gun. By that time I may have located the German machine-gun, so we should be able to knock it out with the Lewis.'

Further speech was cut short by a punctual fantasia from the gun in question. Angus and M'Snape crouched behind the shattered wall, awaiting their chance. The firing ceased.

'*Now!*' whispered Angus.

Next moment officer and corporal were flying across the open, and before the mechanical Boche gunner could jerk the new belt into position, both had found sanctuary within the open doorway of the half-ruined *estaminet*.

Nay, more than both; for as the panting pair flung themselves into shelter, a third figure, short and stout, in an ill-fitting kilt, tumbled heavily through the doorway after them. Simultaneously a stream of machine-gun bullets went storming past.

'Just in time!' observed Angus, well pleased. 'Bogle, what are you doing here?'

'I was given tae unnderstand, sirr,' replied Mr. Bogle calmly, 'when I jined the regiment, that in action an officer's servant stands by his officer.'

'That is true,' conceded Angus; 'but you had no right to follow me against orders. Did you not hear me say that no one but Corporal M'Snape was to come?'

'No, sirr. I doubt I was away at the 'phone.'

'Well, now you are here, wait inside this doorway, where you can see Sergeant Mucklewame's party, and look out for signals. M'Snape, let us find that machine-gun.'

The pair made their way to the hitherto blind side of the building, and cautiously peeped through a much-perforated shutter in the living-room.

'Do you see it, sirr?' inquired M'Snape eagerly.

Angus chuckled.

'See it? Fine! It is right in the open, in the middle of the street. Look!'

He relinquished his peep-hole. The German machine-gun was mounted in the street itself, behind an improvised barrier of bricks and sandbags. It was less than a hundred yards away, sited in a position which, though screened from the view of Angus's platoon farther down, enabled it to sweep all the ground in front of the position. This it was now doing with great intensity, for the brief public appearance of Angus and M'Snape had effectually converted intermittent into continuous fire.

'We must get the Lewis gun over at once,' muttered Angus. 'It can knock that breastwork to pieces.'

He crossed the house again, to see if any of Mucklewame's men had arrived.

They had not. The man with the Lewis gun was lying dead halfway across the street, with his precious weapon on the ground beside him. Two other men, both wounded, were crawling back whence they came, taking what cover they could from the storm of bullets which whizzed a few inches over their flinching bodies.

Angus hastily semaphored to Mucklewame to hold his men in check for the present. Then he returned to the other side of the house.

'How many men are serving that gun?' he said to M'Snape. 'Can you see?'

'Only two, sirr, I think. I cannot see them, but that wee breastwork will not cover more than a couple of men.'

'Mphm,' observed Angus thoughtfully. 'I expect they have been left behind to hold on. Have you a bomb about you?'

The admirable M'Snape produced from his pocket a Mills grenade, and handed it to his superior.

'Just the one, sirr,' he said.

'Go you,' commanded Angus, his voice rising to a more than usually Highland inflection, 'and semaphore to Mucklewame that when he hears the explosion of *this*' – he pulled out the safety-pin of the grenade and gripped the grenade itself in his enormous paw – 'followed, probably, by the temporary cessation of the machine-gun, he is to bring his men over here in a bunch, as hard as they can pelt. Put it as briefly as you can, but make sure he understands. He has a good signaller with him. Send Bogle to report when you have finished. Now repeat what I have said to you. . . . That's right. Carry on!'

M'Snape was gone. Angus, left alone, pensively restored the safety-pin to the grenade, and laid the grenade upon the ground beside him. Then he proceeded to write a brief letter in his field message-book. This he placed in an envelope which he took from his breast pocket. The envelope was already addressed – to the *Reverend Neil M'Lachlan, The Manse*, in a very remote Highland village. (Angus had no mother.) He closed the envelope, initialled it, and buttoned it up in his breast pocket again. After that he took up his grenade and proceeded to make a further examination of the premises. Presently he found what he wanted; and by the time Bogle arrived to announce that Sergeant Mucklewame had signalled 'message understood', his arrangements were complete.

'Stay by this small hole in the wall, Bogle,' he said, 'and the moment the Lewis gun arrives tell them to mount it here and open fire on the enemy gun.'

He left the room, leaving Bogle alone, to listen to the melancholy rustle of peeling wall-paper within and the steady crackling of bullets without. But when, peering through the improvised loophole, he next caught sight of his officer, Angus had emerged from the house by the cellar window, and was creeping with infinite caution behind the shelter of what had once been the wall of the *estaminet*'s back-yard (but was now an uneven bank of bricks, averaging two feet high), in the direction of the German machine-gun. The gun, oblivious of the danger now threatening its right front, continued to fire steadily and hopefully down the street.

Slowly, painfully, Angus crawled on, until he found himself within the right angle formed by the corner of the yard. He could go no further without being seen. Between him and the German gun lay the cobbled surface of the street, offering no cover whatsoever except one mighty shell-crater, situated midway between Angus and the gun, and full to the brim with rain-water.

A single peep over the wall gave him his bearings. The gun was too far away to be reached by a grenade, even when thrown by Angus M'Lachlan. Still, it would create a diversion. It was a time bomb. He would . . .

He stretched out his long arm to its full extent behind him, gave one mighty overarm sweep, and with all the crackling strength of his mighty sinews, hurled the grenade.

It fell into the exact centre of the flooded shell-crater.

Angus said something under his breath which would have shocked a disciple of Kultur. Fortunately the two German gunners did not hear him. But they observed the splash, fifty yards away, and it relieved them from *ennui*, for they were growing tired of firing at nothing. They had not seen the grenade thrown, and were a little puzzled as to the cause of the phenomenon.

Four seconds later their curiosity was more than satisfied. With a muffled roar the shell-hole suddenly spouted its liquid contents and other débris straight to the heavens, startling them considerably and entirely obscuring their vision.

A moment later, with an exultant yell, Angus M'Lachlan was upon them. He sprang into their vision out of the descending cascade – a towering, terrible, kilted figure, bareheaded and berserk mad. He was barely forty yards away.

Initiative is not the *forte* of the Teuton. Number One of the German gun mechanically traversed his weapon four degrees to the right and continued to press the thumb-piece. Mud and splinters of brick sprang up round Angus's feet; but still he came on. He was not twenty yards away now. The gunner, beginning to boggle between waiting and bolting, fumbled at his elevating gear, but Angus was right on him before his thumbs got back to work. Then indeed the gun spoke out with no uncertain voice, for perhaps two seconds. After that it ceased fire altogether.

Almost simultaneously there came a triumphant roar lower down the street, as Mucklewame and his followers dashed obliquely across into the *estaminet*. Mucklewame himself was carrying the derelict Lewis gun. In the doorway stood the watchful M'Snape.

'This way, quick!' he shouted. 'We have the Gairman gun spotted, and the officer is needing the Lewis!'

But M'Snape was wrong. The Lewis was not required.

A few moments later, in the face of brisk sniping from the houses higher up the street, James Bogle, officer's servant – a member of that despised class which, according to the *bandar log* at home, spends the whole of its time pressing its master's trousers and smoking his cigarettes somewhere back in billets – led out a stretcher party to the German gun. Number One had been killed by a shot from Angus's revolver. Number Two had adopted Hindenburg tactics, and was no more to be seen. Angus himself was lying stone-dead a yard from the muzzle of the gun which he, single-handed, had put out of action.

His men carried him back to the *Estaminet Aux Bons Fermiers*, with the German gun, which was afterwards employed to good purpose during the desperate days of attacking and counter-attacking which ensued before the village was finally secured. They laid him in the inner room, and proceeded to put the *estaminet* in a state of defence – ready to hold the same against all comers until such time as the relieving division should take over, and they themselves be enabled, under the kindly cloak of darkness, to carry back their beloved officer to a more worthy resting-place.

In the left-hand breast pocket of Angus's tunic they found his last letter to his father. Two German machine-gun bullets had passed through it. It was forwarded, with a covering letter, by Colonel Kemp. In the letter Angus's commanding officer informed Neil M'Lachlan that his son had been recommended posthumously for the highest honour that the King bestows upon his soldiers.

But for the moment Mucklewame's little band had other work to occupy them. Shelling had recommenced; the enemy were mustering in force behind the village; and presently a series of counter-attacks were launched. They were successfully repelled, in the first instance, by the remainder of 'A' Company, led in person by Bobby

Little, and, when the final struggle came, by the Battalion Reserve under Major Wagstaffe. And throughout the whole grim struggle which ensued, the *Estaminet Aux Bons Fermiers*, tenanted by some of our oldest friends, proved itself the head and corner of the successful defence.

From: *Carrying On – After The First Hundred Thousand.*

IAN HAY (Sir John Hay Beith) was born in 1876, and was educated at Fettes College and St John's, Cambridge University. He was commissioned in the Argyle and Sutherland Highlanders, in which he rose to the rank of Lieutenant-Colonel and was awarded the M.C. and the C.B.E. His first war book, *The First Hundred Thousand*, published in 1915, won wide patriotic acclaim. Three more followed, and after the war he wrote several successful plays. He died in September 1952.

KILLED IN ACTION

Herbert Read

A man dwells in a security of darkness – the inner darkness of sleep and the outer darkness of the dug-out. But not for long. At 7.20 a.m. the earth he dwelt in began to throb with a dull incessant tremor, like the piston-pounding of some infernal engine in the black bowels of Earth. Hammers of Vulcan. Piston-throbs of the revolving world.

Louder were the intermittent kraoump, kraoump of nearer shells falling, marking the time of this infernal symphony.

Kraoush! Danvers hurtled in darkness like a diver from a height into a wet dark sea. That one was near! He could hear the débris falling in a shower at the dug-out entrance. Then he felt the tremor of the ground and heard the kraoump – kraoump. Hell! A barrage. He must get up. His limbs were cold and numb, and his clothes were clammy cold: he had had them on for goodness knows

An Australian officer wading his way through the knee-deep slush that swamped this trench at Guedecourt, December 1916.

how long. The stink of that shell penetrated into the dug-out. He fumbled for a match, and whilst he fumbled the sergeant-major came in with a light. His face was shiny and excited and his contracted pupils rolled about like beads on a white saucer.

'We're for it,' he cried, as he stuck the candle on the shelf. 'The buggers are pelting us like hell. S.O.S. on right and left. Shall I put ours up?'

'Yes.' Danvers lurched off the wire bed-frame. His teeth chattered and he couldn't stop them. Involuntary shivers passed down his body. He must control himself: he must go out and see his men. Set an example. Duty. He sipped a tot of rum and felt its flame within his belly. He reached for his tin-hat and his revolver.

This damned Salient! But you can't expect a soft time always, and they had had six months down Arras way. They knew they were for it when they came north. Now evidently they had got it. The previous night they had relieved the remnants of a battalion which had attacked and taken the ridge they now held. And this was the not unexpected counter-attack.

His battalion was the right battalion of the division. His right rested on a sunken road which pierced the line at right-angles. On his left was 'C' Company. Then the next battalion held the scarred stumps of a wood: Devil's Wood. 'D' Company, with Flint in command, held a position seven hundred yards behind at the foot of the ridge.

Danvers emerged into the riotous open. The earth was in eruption. An almost uniform din, compounded of separate heavy detonations, quivered in the air. The earth gushed up in sudden sprays. Bitter smoke clouds drifted down into the valley, obscuring all but the immediate environment. Ah! The shell that had awakened him fell there. Three untidy inert corpses. There was no regular trench to proceed along; just a ragged joining of shell-holes. He stumbled towards the right. Baistow would be there with his platoon. A reliable fellow, Baistow. Liked by the men. There was an infernal babbling of machine-guns on the right. The Boche must be in sight there. If so, the barrage would be lifting. Our barrage was damned poor. Eugh! Dudd! A great heavy ball of blood shot to his gullet as he drew his body taut to receive the expected detonation. The thing furrowed the ground not two yards from his feet. Harmless enough. But God! What a fright. Did he duck? Well, it was only natural. He looked at his men. They lay cowering on their bellies, their throbbing hearts pressed to the slimy soil. A shell burst fifty yards further on. It must be in the trench. Might as well go on. Next one might drop where I stand now. All a matter of chance.

He came to the crater of that last shell. Yes, poor fellows, two or three lay bleeding, débris among débris. And God, yes, Baistow. Rolled up like a kitten, but dead, most evidently dead.

A sudden cry on the right. Fierce fusillade. A hatless, bleeding man running towards him. Yes? 'Fritz coming down the road behind us': that was intelligible above the din. The division on the right had given way. Now they were outflanked. God, the case looked hopeless! He drew his revolver. No good leaving all these men where they were. He detailed a Lewis-gun team to cover the road. They wouldn't be seen again, but that couldn't be helped. Good death – saving their mates. They might get captured. He gave orders for the rest to withdraw to the left. There was a bank further down that switched off behind them. They might make a protecting flank there. The barrage had now ceased on the front line. They were pounding the supports. Poor Flint.

They got back to the bank, about twenty of them. The two platoons on the left seemed to be all right so far. No sign of any Boches in front. The thought had hardly completed itself when a flight of machine-gun bullets came whistling overhead *from the left rear.* Devil's Wood had gone! The plan was clear now. Their front was to be taken by outflanking tactics. They were almost surrounded. They must hold on until the counter-attack was launched. He sent a runner back to Headquarters with a message: they couldn't hold out for long: the counter-attack must be immediate.

They crouched on the trembling earth, waiting. The barrage had died down considerably on the right. All objectives gained, no doubt. On the left it was as riotous as ever. He looked at his watch. Ten o'clock. For two hours and forty minutes he had been unconscious of time: he had existed in a different duration, a duration measured in agonies.

A sudden uproar of machine-guns and rifles. After all, they were making a frontal attack. There on the left, hundreds of them, their advance covered by the machine-guns in Devil's Wood. No shells. Multitudinous crackling and burr of rifle-fire. There! Half-left, over the crest, they came. Hundreds. His Lewis-gun on the left opened on them. He could see them falling; now one, then two or three in a heap. The Lewis-gun suddenly stopped. Stoppage? Or the team knocked out? He couldn't tell. The guns in Devil's Wood were sweeping along the line. They tremblingly crouched into their shallow shelters. The enemy came on. On the left they were in the line. He could see a few men running back. Others surrendering, overwhelmed. It was bloody. There was no movement on the right. On the left by now the Boches were in possession as far as the junction of Danvers' switch line with the main line. He could see a Boche helmet, not two hundred yards away.

The rifle fire had died away. Then our barrage opened on the old line. Damnably near to them. The shells were falling as near as twenty yards in front of Danvers. They must be right on the fellows further on the left.

There was only one thing to be done. The bank they held made the dip of the slope behind pretty steep and hollow. Ten yards further down and they would be in 'dead' ground. It was worth chancing. And as they were they would only be captured or blown to hell by their own artillery. But they must not go in a body: they must trickle down one by one. He made his intention known to a corporal who was sharing a shell-hole with him. There were a few men nearer the line who wouldn't get down. Still, the enemy were crouching in terror of the descending shells. The corporal crept out to the right: Danvers went to the left. There was no difficulty in getting his intention known. The men were very uneasy at the nearness of the shells, and most of them had already formed the intention: they were only waiting for the lead.

Danvers reckoned there were about fifteen got safely down. There could not have been many more to come.

From the hollow of the slope it was about 150 yards to the line held by the support companies. They paused to get their breath and nerve. Then they trickled across.

Danvers stumbled right on to Flint. They clasped hands, but didn't say anything. Danvers lay back exhausted.

Shortly afterwards they received orders to make a counter-attack at 5 p.m. in conjunction with the troops on the left and right. The ——th Brigade had been ordered up to reinforce the counter-attack, but it was doubtful if it would be in position by that time. At any rate, at five o'clock they must go forward with the remainder of the line.

A strange but blessed stillness came over the scene, as though the guns had vomited themselves to death. The men lay on the wet earth, some of them listlessly eating food they happened to possess.

Danvers had sunk into a dazed reverie, sleepless and bitter. The day's riot still tingled in his brain: his tingling brain lurched like a pendulum, but without forcing into action his volitional machinery. An image would present itself without, however, getting gripped in any process of thought. The past was a remote elusive mirage. The present was mechanical. He chewed some tinned beef, but without sensation or appetite. He answered Flint's questions monosyllabically.

He gradually sank into a stupor, a tense unconsciousness. Then suddenly he awoke. Flint was there with him, writing out a message. The sky was uniformly grey and dull. He arose and stretched his numb limbs.

From his position he could see the whole of the shallow valley stretching to Devil's Wood on the left horizon. All was black and upriven. In the valley the shell-holes were full of water and reflected the harsh cold sky. Devil's Wood was a naked congregation of shattered trunks, like an old broken comb against the skyline. An emotion – a sudden realization and anger – flushed his brain. This was his earth, earth of green slopes, earth of lithe green trees, earth of vigorous sap and delicate growth.

Now riven and violated; a wide glabrous desolation; a black diseased scab, erupted and pustulous. The black shell-holes were like earthy lips puckered to kiss – lips of Mother Earth, incestuously desirous – parched sucking lips eager for his wet red blood.

He looked at his watch. 4.30. The reinforcements ought to be here if they were going to be any good. No time to get into position. They would have to attack without them. Flint was getting the men ready. He must help Flint.

4.45. Our barrage was to come down at 4.50. No reinforcements. If the people on the right were strong enough, perhaps all would be right.

He joined Flint. 'We'll stick together, old man.' 'Rather.'

The guns opened. The first salvo hurtled and screamed above their heads, followed immediately by the rolling detonations.

'They're dropping short!' The majority of the shells were falling half-way between their position and the enemy's.

'Not thick enough,' shouted Flint.

'No damned good at all.'

The retaliation opened. The arched trajectories crossed. Explosive babel.

'Three more minutes,' shrieked Flint, showing his watch.

Danvers nodded.

Time. The barrage would be lifting.

'Now, men!'

They left their shallow defences. Danvers looked over the valley. All the way across men were walking forward, rather scattered, like flies crawling across a side of bacon in a grocer's shop.

They were all right for two hundred yards: dead ground of the hollow slope.

On the crest they would meet the machine-guns. Doesn't matter. Clench your teeth.

God, how forlorn they looked! Flies on bacon.

The crest now. The crest now. They would take it walking. Bodies pitched forward as in a hailstorm.

They had got it on the left. An infernal racket of machine-guns and rifles. Getting nearer. Sweeping. Sweeping nearer, like a breeze across a cornfield.

The bullets shrilled fiercely above their heads. He saw men

dropping – there on the left. One by one, crumbling on the ground as in some sudden dissolution.

Now for it.

Flint sprang forward with a cry, his right hand flung skywards with its menacing revolver.

'Rush it, lads!'

A bullet hit him in the snout. He fell down, sniggering blood, dying.

Danvers glanced at him. Poor devil. Must go on.

They were in the full blast of it. Get down. Must do it in short rushes now.

Up. Vibrant tang of bullets in flight. Men dropping all over the place. When would his turn come? Let it be soon – soon.

Again. Blind onward drift. Not many left now. The few hesitated, wavered, fell dead. Get down!

There were not a dozen men left within five hundred yards of him. Hopeless. They were only a hundred yards from the line, but it was hopeless. The Boches were sniping now. The last man near him was hit in the head.

All was hopeless. Might as well crouch here in this shell-hole. Getting dark now.

Wedge. Conic wedge. Red conic wedge of pain – it entered between his contracted eyebrows, and there was slowly, decisively driven in by the hovering power of despair.

He rammed his head against the soft crushed earth. The cold shadows of evening deepened cruelly.

Flint. Yes, Flint. Killed. Sniggering blood.

The firing had stopped now. It would soon be dark. He might crawl back then. Alone. Defeated. Damned if he would.

He would die.

He jumped up suddenly, facing the enemy. A wild energy blazed in every gesture. 'Fire, damn you, fire! Kill me, you bloody swine.'

No answer. A man coughed somewhere.

The darkness, mistily blue, deepened.

He sank sobbing to the earth.

Presently he felt the cold. At some time he had unconsciously urinated: he began to feel the discomfort of his sodden breeches.

He stood up again. His revolver dangled heavily on its lanyard. He was suddenly very calm.

He pointed the revolver towards his face. Six neat holes, death ready to leap from their clean neat lips. He curled his index finger round the trigger. He was beautifully conscious of the finger's smooth movement – of the small contracting muscles. He curled and opened it a few times.

A squeezing motion, you remember.

He saw the hammer move slowly away from him. A squeezing motion. Infinitely slow retrogression of hammer, the striking-pin a thin sinister black tooth.

A sudden snap and nothing else. A misfire. His eyes opened wide with the agony of a sudden unleashed tension of will. His strained hands trembled. His parched throat emitted a scream.

He stared and screamed at the six neat black holes before his face. Unconsciously he was again squeezing the trigger. The hammer moved back, gaping with its one black tooth. A sinister grimace. Motion of inevitable intent.

The night, hitherto secretly stealing towards him, made a sudden leap to devour his life with blackness and annihilation.

From: *Ambush*: Criterion Miscellany, No. 16.

SIR HERBERT READ was born in Yorkshire in 1893 and was educated at Crossley's School, Halifax, and Leeds University. He served with the Green Howards, 1915–18, on the Western Front, when he was mentioned in dispatches, and was awarded the M.C. and D.S.O. He became a senior Treasury Civil Servant in 1919, before starting an academic career as a Professor of fine arts and poetry in 1922. Editor of the *Burlington Magazine* from 1933 to 38, he has published *Naked Warriors* (1919), *Collected Poems* (1946), as well as several volumes of art history and criticism.